THINGS

Look for all the books in the

VISITORS

trilogy:

VISITORS

THINGS

BOOK II

Rodman Philbrick and Lynn Harnett

AN
APPLE
PAPERBACK

SCHOLASTIC INC.
New York   Toronto   London   Auckland   Sydney

ISBN 0-590-97214-6

12 11 10 9 8 7 6 5 4 3 2   7 8 9/9 0 1 2/0

Printed in the U.S.A.   40
First Scholastic printing, August 1997

To Robert Harnett

1

There are things under the earth that want to eat our brains. Slimy things with tentacles. Things that glow in the dark invading your nightmares. Invading your bedroom. Invading your brain.

This was what I was thinking as I stood in the night looking up at the dark skies over Harley Hill.

Our lives had changed forever the night the aliens blasted out of space, landing in the barren Harley Hills just outside of town and burrowing down into the biggest hill. There had been a tremendous thunderstorm that night, with glowing rain and clouds that boiled with light.

We — me and my twin sister, Jessie — thought it was kind of cool. Until we discovered the aliens had turned our parents into sleepwalking zombies. They kept saying, "Everything-is-perfectly-normal," in their flat robot voices when everything was horribly weird and scary.

The worst of it was, we had no one to turn to for

help. All the adults in Harleyville had become zombie servants of the alien mothership buried under Harley Hill.

It was just us — me and Jessie and our best bud Frasier Wellington. Three twelve-year-old kids against alien invaders trying to take over our town and then — the world!

I shuddered, picturing for an instant all we'd been through — the slithering thing in our parents' alien eyes, the winding melted rock walls of the alien tunnels beckoning us on to the pool of goo, the slimy tentacles snapping as they chased us —

A hand grasped my shoulder and I jumped.

"Nick, are you okay?" asked Jessie. Being twins, sometimes she can almost read my mind.

"Let's get out of here," I said. "Before they come back."

Jess didn't have to ask me who I was talking about. She knew. Them. The *things*.

"Come on, Frasier, we're out of here."

Our best friend Frasier was sitting on the rockslide covering the alien cave opening.

The three of us had made that rockslide happen. It was a huge avalanche burying everything, even the glow of light the aliens had sent out over our town. That rockslide was all that kept the aliens from swallowing up the Harleyville adults who'd been marching right toward it, their minds wiped away.

Part of me wanted to think we were safe now, that

the things under the earth would no longer be mind-melting our parents.

But in my heart I knew the space creatures couldn't be stopped by an avalanche. Not for long. The tentacled monsters would burrow out from under the rockslide. The strange, glowing light from Harley Hills would turn the adults into sleepwalking zombies again.

The visitors were here, and we couldn't stop them.

"Frasier?" Jessie squinted up the hill, looking doubtfully at our friend.

Usually Frasier talks a mile a minute, telling us his scientific theories, or coming up with some crazy scheme. But he was just sitting. His face was a funny granitelike color and he was as still as stone.

"Anything wrong?" Jessie asked him.

"Wrong? Nothing-is-wrong," he said in a flat robotic voice. "Everything-is-perfectly-normal."

He sounded just like our parents after the alien mind-melt!

"You're kidding, right?" I said. "This is one of your stupid jokes."

Instead of laughing or smiling, he just looked at me. And that's when I saw the slithering thing behind Frasier's eyes.

My best friend had just been taken over by the aliens!

"Frasier, snap out of it!" Jessie pleaded.

His head turned in her direction. He stood up and moved his lips into a gross, rubbery-looking smile. He started walking, stiff-legged, toward Jess.

"Come-with-me," he said to her. "Nothing-to-worry-you. Everything-is-normal. Perfectly-normal. You-will-be-safe-with-me."

Jessie's dark eyes widened. She shuddered so hard her brown hair swung over her shoulders. "Unfunny, Frasier," she said. "Hilarious — not!"

Frasier kept moving toward her, one robotic plodding step at a time, that weird smile pasted on his round face. He didn't seem to notice that his glasses were totally crooked.

"Come-with-me," he chanted. "Urgent."

Jessie's eyes switched to me as she backed away. "Tell me he's kidding, Nick," she said nervously. "This is Frasier's sick idea of a joke, right?"

I shook my head. "I don't think so."

Frasier started marching faster toward Jessie. She backed up into a cliff wall. Her head swung right and left in a panic but there was no place for her to go. Frasier stretched his arms toward her, fingers twitching.

"Frasier!" she cried. "Wake up!"

No reaction. Stomach churning, I picked up a small rock. I was too far away to reach him any other way. "Frasier, here!" I called and tossed it at him underhand, like a softball.

Startled, he whipped around, putting his hands up to protect his face. Jessie ran. Frasier's foot skidded on the pebbly ground. He wheeled his arms to keep from falling but his foot went out from under him.

THUD!

His body hit the ground heavily and Frasier began to roll down the hill, faster and faster every second.

"AAAAAAAIIIIIIIIIEEEE — !"

Then his head struck a rock and his scream cut off instantly. His body rolled and came to a stop. He lay there limp, arms flung out, still as death.

2

Jessie and I ran toward Frasier's unmoving body. Our feet slipped and skidded over the rough, steep surface. My blood zinged with fear for Frasier and fear that Jessie and I were both going to take a header right down the hill.

Tentacles would come creeping over all three of us and we wouldn't even know it.

Jessie reached Frasier first. She dropped down by his side and reached out to touch him. "Frasier!" she called urgently, her voice near tears.

My heart leaped into my throat. "NO, Jessie!" I shouted. "Stay back!" What if the alien inside our friend was faking, just waiting for us to come close enough to —

I skidded to a stop beside Jessie, chest heaving. Frasier's face was pasty in the moonlight. His mouth was slack and his glasses twisted over one ear. No way was he faking. But at least he was breathing.

I picked up his head gently and Jessie parted his hair.

There was a nasty lump but it wasn't bleeding. He stirred and groaned. "Owwwww."

Frasier opened his eyes and I stiffened, searching his eyes for the slithering thing I'd seen in my parents' eyes. But it wasn't there.

Pushing himself up, Frasier rubbed his head. "Ow," he said. "I guess these aliens don't have a very good sense of Earth balance. Maybe the gravity on their planet is different."

Jessie let out her breath in relief. "It's really you, now, isn't it, Frasier?"

He nodded and winced. "Weird experience," he said.

"You must have been terrified," I said, leaning against a rock. "What did it feel like?"

"I wasn't scared," said Frasier, trying to straighten his glasses. "It was kind of cool. It was like I was there watching while this weird voice came out of my mouth. It never really had a hold of me. I felt like I could push it out with a flick of my fingers, mentally speaking. But I was interested."

"Interested!?" Jessie cried. "Those slimy things have fifty-foot-long tentacles. They took over the whole town, turned all the adults into zombies, including our own parents in case you didn't notice. After what we did, walling them in with that avalanche, you should have been terrified they'd turn your brain to mush!"

Frasier grinned. "I'm telling you, the thing couldn't really get a handle on me. But you guys! You guys looked *scared*!"

Jessie made a face at him. "Know what, Frasier? You were from another planet even before the alien ate your brain."

Frasier stuck out his tongue and rolled his eyes. Jessie punched his shoulder lightly.

But I was thinking. "Maybe we could learn something from this," I said. "Those things are still there, under Harley Hill. We blocked their tunnel, sure, but it won't stay that way for long. We have to be ready for them. They'll find a way out. And when they do —"

Suddenly Frasier stiffened. "Earth-will-submit," he said in that flat, robotic voice.

Jessie and I sprang back. Shivery chills raced up my spine.

"Everything-will-be-normal," Frasier stated, baring his teeth. "Perfectly-normal."

3

"AAAAH!" cried Jessie, backing away.

I couldn't make a sound. My brain felt frozen.

Frasier boomed out laughing. "Ha, ha, ha, ha." He slapped his knee, and his glasses slid down his nose. "You should see your faces," he said between bursts of laughter. "You guys are so easy!"

Jessie looked murderous, which was about how I felt. She turned and stalked off down the hill, which was hard to do since it was so steep. "I'm going home," she yelled back.

Frasier scrambled to his feet. "It was just a joke," he called out. He looked at me and shrugged. "I thought we could all do with a laugh."

Maybe I was crazy, too, but suddenly it did seem funny. I laughed so hard I almost fell on the ground.

But when I stopped laughing the hills suddenly seemed too quiet. "We'd better catch up to Jessie," I said.

Frasier nodded. But as we started down he looked

around, a puzzled look on his face. "Hey, Nick, where did everybody go?" he asked. "Weren't there like a million people here just a little while ago?"

My heart skipped. He was right. How could I forget all the adults? We'd followed them up here, unable to shake them out of the zombie trance that was pulling them to the aliens' cave.

After the rockslide the aliens had lost their hold on them. The adults had awakened and come back to themselves.

But they'd been horribly confused. They all started wandering aimlessly, uncertain about where they were and where they wanted to go.

Now the hills were empty, except for us.

We hurried down the hill. Jessie was waiting for us where we'd left our bikes. "It's awfully quiet," she whispered, her brown eyes big and anxious in the moonlight. "Does it seem too quiet to you?"

The back of my neck prickled. "It's night," I answered. "It's always quiet at night."

"We'll probably catch up to the adults on the way to town," said Frasier. "They can't be that far ahead of us."

We got on our bikes and rode in silence. The rocky hills cast huge spooky shadows and I couldn't shake the feeling that something was waiting for us in each pool of darkness.

But nothing moved.

"Look!" cried Jessie, pointing to the sky.

My stomach lurched but it was only a flock of birds and they were far away — no danger to us.

"Since when do starlings fly at night?" muttered Frasier.

"They're too far away to tell what they are," I said sharply. "They could be any kind of bird."

"No. I can tell by how they fly," Frasier said quietly. "Starlings."

"They're going so fast," said Jessie, her voice sounding fearful in the dark. "They look like they're fleeing the town as fast as they can."

I shivered uneasily. "Let's not get spooked," I said.

We left the dusty, treeless hills. The road to town led through a wooded area. Hardly any moonlight filtered through the trees. It was so dark we had to slow to a crawl.

Still no people. And no more birds or any other animals either.

But finally the trees began to thin and we saw a few houses, then a few more. All were dark. Nothing stirred on the streets. Harleyville was like a ghost town.

"What's that noise?" asked Frasier, stopping his bike.

There was a rumble in the air and a snuffling noise, too. It sounded like an elephant with a very bad cold.

"It sounds alive," breathed Jessie. "And big."

"It's coming from that house," I said, pointing to the one on my right.

"No," said Frasier. "That one." He pointed to the one across the street.

"It's all of them! All the houses," cried Jessie. She dropped her bike in the road and dashed for the nearest house. "I'm going to find out!" she called as she ran.

"No, don't!" I yelled, but she was already up the porch stairs. She yanked open the front door without even knocking and darted inside.

"Jessie!" I shouted.

All around us the noise seemed to get louder. Hungrier.

4

Frasier and I leaped off our bikes and chased after Jessie. Had the aliens made her do this? Were they waiting inside for us, too?

As we pounded up the porch steps, I saw a dark figure lurking beyond the front door. My breath caught in my throat. Did they already have Jessie?

"Watch out!" I warned Frasier. "I saw something inside."

I grabbed the knob of the screen door and it was instantly jerked out of my hand. The door flew open and something came at me out of the dark house.

"YAH!" I blurted and stumbled backward into Frasier.

"Hey, it's only me," whispered Jessie. "Quiet. Everybody's asleep. Listen."

The snuffling, rumbling noise was really loud. It seemed to shake the house. "Snoring," said Jessie. "They're snoring."

We got back on our bikes and rode slowly toward home. The noise of snoring was unbelievable.

"SSSNNNNNGGGGGGGGGGRRRRRRR —
WWWWWWWWHHHHHHH."

It should have been funny. We should have been rolling in the street, hysterical. But Jessie and Frasier looked as weirded out as I felt.

"How can everybody be sleeping when an hour ago they were all marching to Harley Hill in an alien trance?" wondered Frasier.

"How can everybody be snoring like that?" asked Jessie. "I never heard anything like it. Lots of people never snore."

"And they all sound exactly the same," I said. "That's not normal."

When we reached our house, Frasier came with us to the front door. It was the same here. Loud snores filled the house. My dad snored once in a while but I had never heard Mom snore.

"They sound like train engines going up a real steep hill," said Frasier. "Well, I guess I'll go see if my folks are at it, too."

Jessie and I went inside.

"SSSNNNNNGGGGGGGGGGRRRRRRR —
WWWWWWWWHHHHHHH."

The noise of snoring seemed to shake the walls. "Maybe it's the stress of being taken over by aliens," Jessie suggested.

"Maybe," I said. I was thinking it might be the aliens' way of getting back their strength so they could break out of their new underground prison.

"What should we do now?" Jessie asked.

"What we usually do, I guess." Suddenly I felt exhausted. "Go to our rooms. Get some sleep."

Jessie's eyes locked on mine.

Sleep. It suddenly sounded dangerous.

5

The noise grew louder as we climbed the stairs.

"SSSNNNGGGGGGRRRRRRR —WWWWW-HHHH!"

Mom and Dad were snoring in unison. It was almost like a chant. As if they were summoning something out of the deep.

Jessie clutched my arm. "It's like a spell," she said. "Maybe we should try to wake them. Maybe waking them will break the spell."

We crept down the dark hallway to our parents' room. I pushed open the door and we went in together.

Mom and Dad were lying on their backs. Their bodies were lined up perfectly straight, legs together and arms by their sides outside the covers. Moonlight fell on their faces, making their skin waxy.

"They're like Egyptian mummies," breathed Jessie.

The only thing that showed they were alive was their mouths, making that awful snoring.

"SSSNNGGGGGGRRRRRRR —WWWWW-HHHH!"

Their bodies were as rigid as boards. "If you picked them up with a giant spatula," I said, "I bet they'd stay stiff."

Jessie shivered. Abruptly she leaned over and shook Mom's shoulder. "Mom," she urged. "Wake up. Wake up!"

I moved to the other side of the bed and shook Dad, begging him to wake. But they might have been stone for all the effect we had.

"WAKE UP!" we shouted together, pushing them as hard as we could. "WAKE UP!"

Nothing.

Finally, defeated, my heart cold as ice, I looked up and met Jessie's eyes. I could tell she felt the same. Without a word we turned and left the room.

"We need to sleep," I said, my eyes and limbs suddenly so heavy I could hardly move. "Tomorrow we'll try and figure out what to do."

Jessie yawned. "Right. We need our strength," she said.

We dragged ourselves off to bed, exhausted. But as soon as I lay down, my mind was flooded with horrible images.

A thick, purple tentacle oozing its way through the rockslide, pushing boulders from its path like pebbles. Soon it would reach freedom and its blunt slimy snout would probe the night air for the three kids who had tried to trap it.

More tentacles bubbling out of that strange syrupy pool we'd seen deep inside the aliens' cave. Wiggling and twisting over one another, like a huge pile of worms, all of them looking for us.

I squeezed my eyes shut, trying to force out the pictures but more came. Huge tentacles racing through the streets of town leaving heavy slime trails. Thick gobs of goo pouring in through windows and doors.

The muscles of my arms and legs knotted with fear as I imagined thousands of tentacles wrapping themselves around me, squeezing.

Then suddenly I was wide awake.

TAP, TAP, TAP.

I bolted upright. Something was tapping and scraping at my window. Something was clattering on the roof. My scalp prickled with alarm.

A shadow snaked across my wall. I jumped, my heart racing, before I realized it was just a tree branch.

A big wind had sprung up out of nowhere. It was knocking a tree branch against my window, slapping tiles on the roof. But the night had been quiet and calm. Where had this wind come from?

The house began to creak. The wind gusted even harder and the house moaned in protest.

EEEEEEEEEEEEEEKKKK!

Boards groaned as if a great weight were pressing

down on the house. I heard the timbers of the roof twist. It felt like the house was being blown apart.

Then I had the worst vision of all. Out of the wind flew a huge octopus blob. In my mind I saw it settling over the house, grabbing on with its tentacles. Gobs of purple stuff dripped off it as tentacles burrowed through windows and doors, seeking me.

Above my bed the ceiling creaked loudly and I nearly cried out. I pulled the covers over my head and huddled there in the dark. It was what I used to do as a little kid when I got myself worked up about closet monsters. It had worked then, better than a night-light.

But suddenly the nightmares of my imagination turned real!

I felt a tentacle land on the blanket over my head. It grabbed the edge and yanked the safe cover right off me.

I yelled out! "AAAIIIIEEE!"

A blazing light shined into my eyes. I was blinded!

6

I thrashed in panic and suddenly the light fell away.

"Nick! Stop it! Nick, it's me. Jessica!"

"Jess?" I sat up, blinking. I knew in a minute, when my heart stopped banging my ribs, I'd probably feel foolish.

Jessie retrieved her flashlight from where I'd knocked it to the floor. Her face was white. "Have you looked out the window?" she asked in a tight voice.

"Window?" I turned my head. The moonlight looked brighter. Too bright.

"It's happening again," said Jessie grimly. "Like the first night. The night of the storm."

I jumped out of bed and ran to the window. Jessie was right. Glowing clouds were boiling in the sky over the three rocky peaks of Harley Hills. This was how it had all started.

"At least the clouds aren't moving this way," I said. The first time, the strange clouds had stopped right over our house and unleashed a torrent of glowing pink rain.

20

Everything the rain had touched had been lit up. Like all the trees and leaves and grass and even our old swing set had been brushed with liquid fire.

At the time we had thought it was beautiful.

But the next morning our parents were — different. And there had been that slithering, alien thing behind their eyes. Nothing had been the same since.

"No rain this time either," said Jessie.

Suddenly the whole sky seemed to split open. A jagged bolt of lightning struck the top of Harley Hill — the biggest of the three hills. At the same instant a clap of thunder shook the house. It was so deafening we couldn't hear ourselves scream.

We jumped away from the window and huddled together. "Nick, I think it struck the same spot," whispered Jessie. After that first storm we'd found that lightning had burned a trail all the way down Harley Hill. And last night the alien cave opened at the exact spot the lightning had struck.

"What if it's another spaceship landing to help the ones we buried?" asked Jessica, echoing my own horrified thoughts.

I could feel her arm trembling against me. "Maybe the ones we saw are leaving," I suggested weakly, not even believing it myself.

Instead, I imagined a new swarm of the things, all bent on revenge and capable of taking over human brains.

"Nick, listen!"

I lifted my head but didn't hear anything. The menacing, rainless storm was quieting down, although the clouds still cast that awful yellowish-pink light over the hills. "What?"

"The snoring! It stopped," said Jessie.

My heart lurched between fear and hope. "Maybe the aliens really have gone," I said. Or else they'd regained their strength and —

Jessie gasped. She clutched my arm. We heard heavy marching footsteps in the hall. Coming this way.

THUMP, thump, THUMP, thump, THUMP, thump.

We backed up against the wall and stared at my bedroom door. My blood froze in my veins.

THUMP, thump, THUMP, thump.

7

CREEAK! THUMP, thump, THUMP, thump.

"They're going downstairs," I said, recognizing the creaky sound of the board on the top step.

We both slumped against the wall. We were trembling head to foot. It was horrible to be so afraid of our own parents. But the slithering alien thing in their eyes and the strange robotic way they talked made us afraid they would give us to the aliens.

They weren't our parents. Not anymore.

We crept to my bedroom door and carefully eased it open a crack. We heard them moving around downstairs but no voices.

"It is Mom and Dad, isn't it?" asked Jessie, sounding worried.

CREEEAK. A door opened, slammed shut.

"They're going down in the basement," I said, my heart sinking.

Our parents had spent a lot of time in the basement

since the aliens arrived. Dad was so busy down there he didn't have time to go to work anymore. And Mom, who used to nag us about nutrition, no longer made meals. The basement took up all their time.

We'd heard sounds of digging and heavy things being moved. But we hadn't been allowed down there. They'd even bought a shiny new padlock to keep us out when they weren't there. And a bolt for the inside of the door.

"I have to know what's going on," I said, opening my bedroom door wider and tiptoeing out into the hall.

"I'm coming too," said Jessie.

Mom and Dad hadn't turned on any lights. The house was as dark as a grave. I swallowed the urge to run back and hide my head under the covers.

"Digging." We could hear the scrape of shovels, the bite of the shovels into dirt. But no human noises. No voices, no grunts of effort. It was like machines were doing the work.

"I know they're digging. But *what* are they digging?" Jessie reached a shaky hand toward the doorknob.

I caught my breath, dread pooling in my stomach. "Maybe they're digging our graves."

"Don't say that!" Jessie grabbed the doorknob and twisted. Locked.

"Listen!" I shushed her. Put my ear to the door.

The digging sounds had stopped. All sound had stopped. It was quiet as a tomb down there. Icy cold trickled down my spine. I backed away from the door.

"Even if Mom and Dad *have* been taken over by aliens," Jessie whispered, "they wouldn't hurt us, would they? Would they?"

Suddenly the basement door flew open.

8

Light flooded the kitchen. I flung up an arm to shield my eyes. Jessie cried out.

Two huge black shapes were emerging out of the light.

"Greetings, offspring."

It was Dad. With the light behind him I couldn't see his face. Except for his eyes. They were glowing. With that same yellow-pink light that came from the clouds over Harley Hill.

He stepped into the kitchen and I saw Mom. Her eyes were glowing, too. "Come-with-us," she said in a mechanical voice.

Dad reached out his hands toward me. Flakes of dirt drifted down. His hands were black with dirt. I felt rooted to the floor. His fingers curved into claws and I couldn't move.

Suddenly I was yanked nearly off my feet.

"Run, Nick," yelled Jessie, dragging me by the arm. "Run!"

We fled from the kitchen, our feet barely touching the floor. Behind us we heard a bellow of anger, then heavy running footsteps.

"They're after us," I yelled. Something hit my ankles and I went flying. As I sprawled on the floor I realized I'd tripped over a footstool.

"Ahh." A deep grunt of satisfaction. Fingers closed over my pajama collar. I felt dirt dribble down my back.

"No!" screamed Jessie. She tugged my arm.

The fingers took hold, icy cold against my neck. I got my feet under me, fear pounding in my veins, and twisted away. Jessie pulled and both of us went vaulting over the dining room table.

We scrambled to our feet and, half running, half crawling, stumbled into the living room and huddled behind the couch. "We'll make a run for the door," I whispered. "We've got to get out of this house."

We heard Dad move into the living room and hesitate, uncertain where we'd gone.

"The-door!" Mom called out. "Block-the-door. Don't-let-the-offspring-escape!"

My insides knotted. We were trapped. By our own parents!

Jessie made a tiny whimpering noise. She began to crawl along the back of the couch. "Come on," she whispered.

Staying close to the floor, we crept behind another chair and then made a dash for the den.

"The window," urged Jessie.

It was open but screened. I yanked at the screen. It stuck and I felt the seconds ticking faster as I struggled with it. At last it came free with a loud tearing noise.

I heard a yell from Dad and pelting footsteps. I hoisted Jessie onto the windowsill and she dove out, headfirst, crashing into the bushes below.

I jumped up into the open window, my heart beating so hard I felt it would explode, and launched myself out into the night.

Only I didn't make it.

"Gotcha!"

A hand clamped down on my foot like a vise.

9

I grabbed onto the windowsill with both hands but Dad was stronger. Inch by inch I was pulled back into the house.

"Hold on, Nick," yelled Jessie. She grabbed my shoulders and pulled at me with all her might.

Then I did something I never thought I would do. I kicked my own father.

"Oooomph!" he grunted, and his grip loosened.

I kicked again. *He's not himself*, I told myself. *He doesn't know what he's doing. It's not really Dad.*

My foot connected with his chest. His fingers slipped and I yanked my foot free and tumbled over the sill into the broken bushes, knocking Jessie to the ground.

She was up in an instant, pulling me to my feet. "Run!" she shouted.

We kept to the shadows of the bushes, running in a crouch. We'd gotten as far as the garage when we heard the front door open. Afraid of being seen, we dove into the tall weeds behind the garage.

"Children," called Mom in a fake sweet voice that made my skin crawl. "Come-in-the-house-now. It's-time-you-went-to-your-sleeping-chambers. Nick! Jessie!"

Dad came out behind her and began to search the bushes around the house. We crouched down as low as we could get and tried not to move so much as an eyelid.

"Nick!" he called with the same fake friendliness. "Jessie! Emerge-from-your-hiding-place-immediately!"

Jessie and I pressed against the garage, hardly daring to breathe. Luckily Mom and Dad didn't look for very long. They must have thought we'd run farther away. After a little while they had a conference on the front stoop and went inside.

When the door closed, Jessie leaned close to my ear. "We've got to get out of here," she whispered.

I shook my head. "I don't think we should move," I told her. "I think they're watching from inside. Just waiting for us to show ourselves so they can grab us. We have to outwait them."

Jessie sighed and settled against the garage wall. "You might be right," she said, trying to slap a mosquito without making any noise. "I guess we can't take a chance."

After a while Jessie's breathing evened out in sleep, but my worries kept me awake. I kept hearing our parents' robotic voices in my mind. It gave me the shudders.

How could we help them? How could we save our

town? We needed to defeat the powerful tentacled aliens, but how? We were just kids. They were creatures who could turn people into zombies to do their bidding.

But I must have drifted into sleep finally because my heart nearly jumped out of my chest when a mechanical screaming split the night apart.

WWWWEEEEEEEEEEEEEEEEEWWWWW-WWWEEEEEEEE.

Jessie jumped up yelling, clapping her hands over her ears. The noise stabbed into the center of my brain. It ran down my back like a bolt of lightning and sent shivers through my arms and legs.

Then a huge blinding light came out of the sky to penetrate the weeds where we were hiding. Aliens!? Gasping, we bolted for the street.

More lights — a swirl of flashing blue and red. I was blinded and dizzy and deafened. I could hardly feel Jessie's hand. I tried to see beyond the dizzying glare into the darkness but the whirling lights filled the night.

We ran blindly, hoping we were headed for the street.

Then — WHAM — I ran smack into something huge. It felt cold and hard, like metal. I fell to the street and banged my head on the curb.

The last thing I remembered was the whirling lights dazzling my eyes. A loud burst of static. And a voice from another world, calling me.

10

Something coiled around my waist. I squeezed my eyes shut tight, too petrified to look. Something gripped my legs. I began to rise into the air.

"AAAAAHHH!" In a burst of panic I thrashed wildly. The lights spun behind my closed eyelids.

"Hey, hey, hold it," said a strange man's voice.

I opened my eyes. It was only a man holding me up, his arms cradling my back and legs. A stranger, but normal looking. His expression was concerned. I couldn't see any slithering motion in his ordinary blue eyes.

"Well, I guess you're all right, after all," he said, setting me down. The whirling lights glinted off his police badge. "You ran full tilt into my patrol car," he said. "Nearly knocked yourself out. I'm Officer Trueblood and I've been looking for you two. Your parents are plenty worried."

I rubbed my head, still shaking from the scare. I felt a lift of hope that the man seemed normal. Maybe the aliens had left the police alone.

Jessie was standing on the sidewalk, the police lights flashing like zebra stripes over her worried face.

"We can't go back in there," said Jessie, looking wild-eyed. "Our parents are acting weird. They've, um, they —" She stopped, chewing her lip. I could tell she knew how nuts it would sound to start babbling about aliens.

I looked over my shoulder at our house, wondering why Mom and Dad hadn't come running out. Maybe they'd gone back to the basement.

"I know it sounds crazy," I said to Officer Trueblood. "But we're really scared. Can't you take us to the police station or something and tomorrow we can work this out?"

The policeman looked sympathetic. He had a nice face, broad and friendly. "Well, we'll have to talk to your parents first," he said.

My shoulders slumped.

"But don't worry," Officer Trueblood continued. "I'll be with you and I'll make sure nothing funny is going on. It's my job to make sure you're safe."

Jessie made a sudden move like she was going to run but Officer Trueblood was quicker. The next minute he was holding us each by the shoulder and marching us up the front walk to our house.

The door opened as we climbed the front steps. Mom and Dad stood back from the door, waiting for us with frozen smiles. I saw a slithering motion deep in their eyes as they looked at the officer.

He must see it, too, I thought. *He won't leave us here in their clutches.*

The policeman pushed us inside and stood blocking the door. "Troublesome-offspring-returned," he said in a flat zombielike voice.

My heart tripped. He had tricked us! He was one of them! Jessie threw a desperate look over her shoulder but Mom's arm snaked out and caught her.

Dad's eyes began to glow again with that awful yellowish-pink light. "You-have-disobeyed. You-must-be-punished," he said, talking like a robot. Officer Trueblood nodded, folding his big arms over his chest.

"Please, Dad," I cried, hoping my voice could reach him. "Don't send us to the basement. We're your children. Don't give us to the aliens."

I remembered what Frasier had said about being aware of his alien voice and watching himself. Maybe Mom and Dad were inside there, too, horrified by what was happening to them. Maybe I could reach their real selves and make them break out of the alien grip.

But Dad just frowned, not even looking at me. For a few seconds he didn't say anything and I started to hope. Then he spoke. "You-two-will-go-to-your-cubicles," he said in his flat, robotic voice.

"What?" asked Jessie, twisting her head to look up at Mom.

"Your-bedrooms," Mom said impatiently. "Go-to-your-rooms."

For an instant her eyes glowed brightly, almost hungrily. I shuddered, wondering what their plan was.

Jessie and I hurried toward the stairs, glad to get away from them. As we started up, I glanced back at the adults. Mom and Dad and Officer Trueblood were just standing there looking at each other. Trading glances, like they were talking without speaking.

Their eyes began to glow and the slithering thing was much more noticeable, as if it was crawling to the surface.

The hair on the back of my neck stood up. I bit my lip to keep from crying out. It was best if they didn't notice me.

Officer Trueblood suddenly nodded once, then turned on his heel and went out, closing the door firmly behind him.

Together, Mom and Dad slowly swiveled their heads toward the stairs and us. We nearly fell over our feet in our sudden hurry to get to the top. They walked to the bottom of the stairs and just stood there, looking up at us.

My skin prickled where their gaze touched. They had plans for us. I felt it.

11

Mom and Dad were still standing there when we reached the top of the stairs. I risked a backwards glance. They were motionless and silent, their heads raised at identical angles.

"What do we do now?" Jessie whispered.

"We'll have to go to our rooms," I whispered back. "Just don't go to sleep, whatever you do."

"No danger of that." Jessie shivered. "Nick, tomorrow we'll have to get away from here. Run away. Until we can figure out how to save Mom and Dad."

I nodded but suddenly I was afraid our parents could hear us.

In my room I went to the window. The glow over Harley Hills was gone. Now they just looked cold and rocky. We had played there for years, me and Jessie and Frasier, but now I hated the place.

Harley Hills had always been a little spooky and scary. That was one of the things we had liked about it. But now it seemed like the hills had been waiting for the

36

aliens. It was a perfect base for them. From those rocky isolated hills they could take over a whole town and no one else would know.

Anger flared up in me. I banged my fist on the windowsill, vowing I would keep the aliens from getting me and Jessie. Together we would fight them and free our town.

Then, all of a sudden, my scalp began to prickle. A shiver ran down my spine like a sliver of ice. Dread enveloped me like a damp cold blanket. What was happening to me?

I raised my head and listened, trying to sense what was going on in the house. And then, like a flash going off in my head, I knew.

Something bad was happening to Jessie.

I spun away from the window, trying to throw off the heavy foreboding dragging at me. I had to get to Jessie.

As I moved across the room, I thought I heard rapid sneaking footsteps in the hallway outside. And whispers.

I raced to my door and flung it open. The hall was quiet and dark. No one was there. The loudest noise was my pounding heart.

Slipping out, I ran as quietly as I could along the hall, my ears alert for any sound. Around me the house creaked, making me jump.

Hunched figures hid in the shadows, lurking in wait, making my heart race painfully. But I kept moving, fear for my sister urging me on. Shadows rose over me as I approached. Then dissolved into nothing as I passed.

Reaching Jessie's room, I put my ear to the door. The door swung open, startling me. My heart hammering, I peered into the darkness. Faint moonlight fell over the bed. I could make out a Jessie-size lump under the covers.

She was there! Hiding under the covers. I let out my breath in relief. But I knew we'd had enough of this. The danger was too great to stay here another minute. I'd grab Jessie and we'd escape now.

Crossing the room, I swept the blanket off my sister.

She wasn't there!

It was only two pillows bunched up to look like someone sleeping. Jessie was gone.

But while I stared at those pillows, a door slammed downstairs. The basement door.

12

"Jessie!"

I leaped across the room and raced down the hall to the stairs. But as I started down, my foot caught on something soft. I went flying into the air, seeing the floor a long way below me.

My heart leaped into my throat. I flung up my arms to protect my head, and my foot caught on the banister post. I grabbed the banister and threw my leg over it. As I began a fast slide down, I glimpsed what had tripped me.

It was Morty, Jessie's old one-eyed stuffed rabbit. She never played with it anymore but she still took it to bed sometimes when she was feeling scared or sad.

My chest tightened. I slid the rest of the way down the banister and hit the floor with a hard thump. Ignoring my twisted ankle, I ran for the basement door.

It was locked. But light leaked from underneath it and I could hear noises down there. There was a drag-

ging sound, a grunt, then a muffled cry that could have
been Jessie.

"Noooooo —"

That cry echoed in my head, piercing my heart like a
knife. I pounded on the door, yelling. "MOM! DAD!
JESSIE!" Maybe if I screamed loud enough it would
wake my parents from their horrible trance.

But no one came, no one answered. At last, hoarse
from shouting, I put my ear to the door again. Maybe if
I could figure out what they were doing, I could stop
them.

I heard a shovel bite into dirt and then a voice rang in
my skull.

"NOOOO!" It was Jessie's voice but it wasn't coming
through the door. It was in my head!

Strange feelings pulled at me. Fear, but not my fear. I
fell against the door, then slumped to the floor. I was
too weak to move.

I felt the rough bump of heels dragging against a dirt
floor. It was Jessie! I was feeling what was happening to
my sister.

Paralyzed somehow, she couldn't move. Her terror
churned in my stomach. There was a hood or something over her face so she couldn't see what was happening. She was closed in, the darkness pressed on her.

I felt the sensation of being carried, the hopelessness
of being unable to struggle. My breath strangled in my
throat. I pawed at the basement door as if I really were
Jessie, trying to fight my way free.

Then there was light, bright enough to penetrate the hood. Jessie saw dark formless shapes gathering around her. Terror forced its way up my throat as a glowing *thing* came closer, closer, closer —

I must have passed out then because I came to and Jessie was gone from my mind. My head was propped against the basement door.

Something was coming up from the basement. It had a heavy menacing tread.

It was coming to finish the job. Coming to get me.

13

I scuttled sideways to get away from the door. But not quickly enough. The door flew open.

Mom and Dad looked down on me crouching there on the floor and smiled. Their smiles were horrible.

"Jessie!" I screamed. "What have you done to her?"

They smiled even more broadly and exchanged glances. "The-female-child-is-well. Perfectly-well," they said in unison. "And-soon-she-will-be-normal. Perfectly-normal."

"You gave her to them, to the *things*," I shouted. "You want her turned into an alien, just like you!"

"You-understand-nothing," they said in the same flat, even voice. "But-you-want-to-be-like-your-sister. To-be-with-her. You-want-us-all-to-be-a-perfectly-normal-family."

I felt their voices reach into my mind like scaly fingers. They were trying to hypnotize me!

Mom stepped closer and held out her hand. "Come.

We-will-all-be-together," she said, her eyes boring into mine.

It was horrible. She looked like Mom, she wore the same clothes and had the same shiny brown hair. But there was a slithering thing behind her eyes that had wormed its way into her brain.

"No!" I screamed, pushing myself across the floor with my heels. "No!"

I scrambled to all fours, then to my feet, stumbling as I ran. Their voices followed me like evil echoes of my parents calling. Then I heard them coming after me.

This time I had to beat them to the front door. They'd never give me time to get out of a window again. I knocked a dining room chair into their path and then another as I raced for the living room.

Somersaulting over my dad's favorite armchair, I kicked an end table over to slow them down, sending a lamp and some books flying. The lamp smashed, littering the floor with splinters of glass.

I heard Dad's grunt of pain as he barked a shin on the end table but it didn't slow him down much. Heavy feet crunched the broken glass. I might make the door but it wouldn't take him long to catch up with me.

Then my eyes lit on the jar of marbles I'd left on a shelf by the front door. Mom had never made me put them away — another sign of how changed she was.

With one hand I yanked the front door open.

With the other I grabbed the jar of marbles. I spilled the marbles across the floor behind me and lit out the door.

As I slammed the door behind me I heard Dad cry out and then WHOMP, his full weight hit the floor. I winced but kept running and reached the street before I heard Mom skid on the marbles and fall, too.

But where could I go? Officer Trueblood would be back here in a flash, looking for me. I didn't think the bushes would be shelter enough this time.

Still running, I found myself in front of Frasier's house. It was dark downstairs but there was a light on in Frasier's room. Chest heaving, I crossed the lawn silently and peeked into the downstairs windows.

No one there. The house was quiet.

Jumping up onto the porch railing, I hauled myself up onto the porch roof.

GGGGRRRRRRNNN!

The old roof sagged loudly under me. I froze, expecting to fall right through it.

But the roof held, although the boards under me continued to creak and groan. I crawled up against the house and hunched there, waiting to see if Frasier's parents would come.

The house stayed quiet. No one stirred. After a while I started moving again, pressing myself against the house, sneaking along to Frasier's room. Every step was an agony of noise.

CRRREEEEAK. GGGGRRRRRNNNN.

Finally I reached Frasier's room. The light was still on. Slowly I stood up and looked inside.

Frasier's shadow was a sharp outline against the wall. Yes! It looked like he was hunched over his computer, absorbed in something.

Craning my neck to see over to the computer, I raised my fist to knock on the window.

But — something wasn't right. There was Frasier's computer. But no Frasier.

The computer was off, his chair empty. I looked at the wall. His shadow was still there! Frasier hadn't moved but he wasn't where his shadow showed him to be.

Little currents of alarm began to ripple across my skin. I stood on tiptoes, and my eyes probed the room.

It was empty! No Frasier. Just his shadow. Impossible but true.

What had they done to Frasier?

I pressed my nose to the glass, feeling more alone than ever. My shoulders began to sag with hopelessness.

And then a hand shot out of the dark and grabbed my neck.

14

My feet slid on the porch roof. Boards creaked under me, drowning out my strangled yell.

I pried at the choking fingers. But I was slipping on the roof and my fingers were weak. My throat felt like it was being crushed.

Gurgling, I twisted to get free, bashing out at whatever was on the end of that viselike grip.

"Nick?!"

"Frasier?!"

Frasier's hand fell away from my neck. He climbed down from the roof over his window.

"Wow, man," he said. "I had no idea it was you."

I rubbed my neck. "You have quite a grip, Frasier. I thought I was a goner."

"Sorry." Frasier slumped down beside me under his window. His face was drained of blood and he was shaking all over. "I thought you were an alien. Or one of their human zombie servants come to get me. I heard

46

noises, like someone was sneaking up the side of the house to get at my window."

"Yeah," I said. "Me."

We sat quiet for a few seconds, catching our breath and letting our heartbeats return to normal.

"Say, how'd you like my shadow?" Frasier asked, jumping up to look in his window. "Pretty cool, huh? When I heard the noises, I cut a piece of cardboard to look like my outline and taped it to the wall so it would throw a shadow like I was at my computer. Then I climbed out to wait for the invader."

He pushed up the window and looked at me. "I'm glad it was only you. Hope I didn't hurt you. Let's go in."

We pulled ourselves in through Frasier's window and I noticed Frasier had his door barricaded, a board nailed right across it so it wouldn't open.

"Wow, Frase," I said, staring at it.

He looked grim. "My mom and dad knocked on the door a couple hours ago. They sounded really weird, like they had wooden frogs in their throats. They wanted me to go for a walk. Right! I don't think so."

"I didn't think your parents liked to walk," I said numbly, sitting on the bed.

Frasier took off his glasses and rolled his eyes. "Walk? These are people who get in the car to go to your house," he said. "But that's not the end of it. They tried to drag me — physically — out of my room. I managed to get the door shut and bolted but I knew that little bolt wouldn't hold them for long."

He sighed. "My parents were always weird but now they're *really* strange."

I shivered, thinking of my own parents chasing me through the house, dragging Jessie off to the basement.

"That's because they're not really your parents," I said. "They're being controlled by that thing in the tunnels. You felt it, Frasier. You know how strong it is."

Frasier frowned and shook his head. "It couldn't have made me turn against my parents, I know that."

"That's because you're a kid," I said. "They can't seem to take over our brains like they can adult brains. Our parents might be paralyzed in there, watching everything but helpless to stop it. We've got to save them, Frasier."

"Maybe we should call somebody," said Frasier. "The state police or the FBI or somebody."

"Right, like they're going to believe us," I said. "If you were them who would you believe — a bunch of kids yelling about aliens or a whole town of reasonable adults who can't imagine what's got into us?"

Frasier frowned. "We could show them," he said. "Dig out the rockslide and take them into the tunnel. Show them the glowing pool we found, let them get chased by a slimy tentacle that stretches on forever. They'll believe us then."

"We don't have time for all that, Frase."

His head shot up. I think he knew what I was going to say before I said it.

"They've got Jessie," I told him.

"No way," he breathed, his eyes round behind the thick glasses.

I nodded. "And you're going to help me get her back."

15

Frasier listened to my story without interrupting. As I described what had happened, I felt Jessie's terror once again and suddenly the minutes seemed to be whizzing by like seconds.

"We've got to hurry," I said, jumping up and starting for the window.

"Wait," said Frasier. He knelt down and pulled out a cordless drill, a hammer, and a flashlight.

"We'll need the drill to get through that lock on the basement door," he said. "The flashlight is obvious and a hammer always comes in handy."

We let ourselves out the window and down the porch roof, trying to be as quiet as possible. We crossed the lawn to the street and kept to the shadows as we made our way to my house.

The house was dark. Cold foreboding clutched my heart. Mom and Dad weren't out looking for me or sitting inside waiting for Officer Trueblood to bring me home. That meant they were in the basement.

"Hurry," I urged Frasier. Panic surged through me in sickening waves. Jessie was in terrible trouble. I could feel it.

We crept quickly around the house to the back door. Frasier aimed his drill at the lock, but when I tried the doorknob, I found the door open.

Spooky thoughts flitted into my brain but I pushed them away. So Mom and Dad had forgotten to lock the back door. That didn't mean they were lying in wait for us. It only meant they weren't themselves, but I already knew that.

We let ourselves into the kitchen. No light showed under the basement door. The big padlock was shiny even in the dark. Frasier got ready to drill but when he hefted the lock, it was open. They hadn't locked up. Did that mean they were still down there? In the dark?

The basement door creaked opened at a touch.

Frasier and I looked at each other. The basement yawned before us, a black hole waiting to suck us in.

Frasier switched on his flashlight but the beam hardly penetrated the darkness. We listened hard but there wasn't a sound.

Where were Mom and Dad? I wondered. Had they delivered Jessie to the aliens and gone to bed? Or were they down there, perfectly still, lying in wait for us?

We started down. I avoided the places on the steps that creaked and pointed them out to Frasier. At every step Frasier probed the dark with his light but we saw nothing. It was like the dark was swallowing the light.

CRREEEEAAK —

Frasier lifted his foot instantly but the noise of the creaking step seemed to reverberate through the house and basement. We froze, listening. But nothing moved. There was no sound from above. Or below.

I looked up to where the open basement door should have been but saw nothing. In a sudden panic I grabbed Frasier's arm and shined the light upward. I let out my breath. The door was still open.

But now I couldn't shake the thought that my parents could slam the door shut any second and lock us down here. Finally they had me where they'd wanted me all along.

We started down again. Frasier's light winked out. We were plunged into blackness. My heart skipped. Frasier gasped and shook the flashlight. It came on again but the light was weak, as if the battery was low.

"Don't worry," Frasier whispered in my ear. "I put in a new battery earlier. It should last for hours."

I tried to calm my breathing as we edged down a few more stairs. My foot touched dirt. We had reached the basement. Frasier's light flickered, died.

The darkness was total. As we stood there it seemed to come for us, wrapping our bodies in coils of inky nothingness.

My heart started jerking like a jackhammer. I flailed out my arms and something soft and sticky plopped onto my hand and clung.

"UGGHH —"

Frasier's light winked back on. The clingy thing on my hand was just a cobweb. I scraped my hand on my pants, fighting off a sick feeling in my throat.

Frasier swung the light around. It flickered, then stayed on. But the weak beam held off the darkness for only a few inches.

"I don't understand it," whispered Frasier. "It's a good flashlight. New battery. It doesn't make sense."

"It's as if the darkness is soaking it up," I breathed.

Frasier shivered. "Come on, man. Let's see what's down here."

He moved deeper into the basement. I started after him but almost immediately Frasier disappeared into the blackness. I opened my mouth to call out softly but the darkness filled my mouth and flowed down my throat.

My breath got choppy. I stumbled after Frasier, feeling panic rise up inside me. The dark was sucking away my breath.

I wanted to run back up the stairs but I didn't know which way to turn. My feet were sinking into the dirt floor. I could feel the dirt creep up and swim around my ankles, holding me. My breath was shallow and painful.

"Jessie!" I cried inside my head. A sudden urgency to find her rushed through me but I was helpless. I couldn't move. The dark was swallowing me.

I bumped into something bony. Jerking my hand to

push it away, I touched something cold and damp. It moved. I felt its slimy skin seeking my hand. I wanted to scream but my jaw was locked shut.

The bony skeleton brushed against me.

Then Frasier suddenly cried out and light leaped up around me like tongues of fire.

The clammy thing grabbed my hand.

16

"I found it," shouted Frasier excitedly. "I know where they took Jessie!"

Cold, dim light filled the basement with swaying, flickering shadows. I jerked, knocking the clammy grip from my hand and stumbling backward into the skeleton.

CRR — AACK!

The brittle thing snapped. I whipped around to look behind me. It was no skeleton — only a rickety old wooden chair. But where was the slimy thing I'd felt? Had it been a tentacle, creeping out of the old stone wall?

I looked at the wall but it was solid with no cracks. Then, under the chair I saw something that made my heart stop.

Quickly I bent and picked it up. Damp and slimy with basement mud, it was one of Jessie's sneakers! It must have been lying on the chair where I'd brushed against it.

"Nick!" called Frasier impatiently. "Are you coming or what?"

I looked over at him. He was standing under a bare lightbulb hanging from the rafters by a cord. The bulb swung, making shadows leap out at us from the walls.

"Lucky I bumped into this," he said, indicating the lightbulb. "Or I never would have found the tunnel."

I hurried over. Shovels leaned against the stone wall. More stones were stacked along the edge of the wall. Piles of dirt were humped all around us, piled almost as high as the low ceiling.

And behind Frasier, part of the wall was gone. In its place was the opening to a tunnel. The light from the bulb didn't shine into the tunnel at all.

We stooped over and peered in. Frasier pointed his flashlight beam inside but all we could see was dirt and darkness. We heard dirt sift down from the tunnel ceiling.

"Think it's safe?" asked Frasier doubtfully.

Without answering, I stepped inside the tunnel.

Instantly I could feel the walls and floor and ceiling pressing down. Tons and tons of dirt, ready to cave in and smother me. I knew how it would feel as the dirt rose up around me and rained down on my head, trapping me. Dirt would pack into my nostrils and fill my throat —

Suddenly another picture entered my mind, clearer

than anything. A body, lying rigid in the darkness. Jessie!

"Maybe we should go back for another flashlight," Frasier suggested. His voice sounded far away.

"No time," I said hoarsely. "Jessie's in danger."

I started down the tunnel, my twin sister's feelings pulling me along. Her fears tumbled around in my head. Confusion. She didn't know what was happening to her.

We had to crouch as we went, the tunnel was so low. Frasier's flashlight hardly lit more than a few inches ahead. Dirt sifted down onto our heads, dribbled down inside our shirts.

I felt the weight of the earth surrounding us.

The flashlight began to flicker again. It went out. The darkness here was even worse than the basement. Dark probed and pushed at us. It wrapped us in hungry arms that tightened around our throats, cutting off air.

When the light came back on my heartbeat was thundering in my ears.

"Maybe this isn't such a good idea," said Frasier. "We're not very well prepared."

But I could feel Jessie in my mind. She was so afraid. And she felt so terribly alone. I felt her clinging to one thought, one thought that was keeping her sane. *Nick will come,* she told herself. *Nick will help me.*

And I would. Or die trying.

"Jessie's down here," I told Frasier. "I can feel it."

"You know where we're headed, don't you?" he asked in a quaking voice.

I nodded but of course he couldn't see in the dark. "Harley Hills," I said. "We're headed straight for Harley Hills."

17

After a while our necks and shoulders were so strained from bending, we almost forgot to be scared. Almost.

Every time the flashlight flickered out, panic grabbed us. The dark was like a living thing, its hungry breath cold on our necks. But we were safe, as long as the light held out.

Frasier would bang the flashlight on his knee and the weak beam would shine again and the dark would shrink back from us.

"Is it my imagination," asked Frasier, "or are we going deeper?"

"I don't know," I said, my voice sounding hollow. But it seemed to me that the earth pressed harder on us. My heart felt squeezed. A growing dread was stealing over me, almost drowning out the feel of Jessie in my mind.

"Hear that?" asked Frasier.

"What?" I listened and then I heard it, too. A deep

steady hum, like the lowest note of a church organ. It pulled at the dread in me, coiling it tight around my lungs so that I could hardly breathe.

It was the hum we'd followed into the aliens' cave, the hum that came loudest from the heart of the cave. When we caused the rockslide the low hum had stopped. But now it was back.

"We must be close," I said, struggling to get the words out of my closing throat.

Frasier's light winked out again and then — SMACK! I ran into something hard and solid. I sprang back, biting down on a scream. Blood thundered in my ears. "The light," I begged. "Get the light on."

Frasier shook the flashlight and banged it against his leg. Finally a small flickering beam played across the thing in front of me.

"A wall!" I exclaimed.

Cautiously we moved forward. "It looks like rock has been melted across the tunnel," said Frasier. "We'll never get through that. But it doesn't make sense. Why build a tunnel just to block it up here?"

"I think it's a door," I told him. "But we don't have the key. Or the mind power to melt it."

We felt the whole length and width of it but it was smooth and glassy. There were no handholds or cracks anywhere.

"What do we do now?" Frasier asked.

"Something wants to keep us out," I said, scraping my fingers frantically along the rock. "Maybe that means we have a chance. Jessie is on the other side of that wall. I can feel her. We've got to get to her."

"Any ideas how?" asked Frasier.

"We'll have to go back. Try to get in from the other side," I said, my heart sinking. But I knew it was the only way. "From the Harley Hills side."

The trip back was horrible. With every step I felt Jessie slipping away. But at least the flashlight didn't die until we were back in the basement — and no one was waiting for us at the end of the tunnel.

No one stopped us as we sneaked out of the house and got our bikes.

We rode through streets that were totally silent and still. Dawn was beginning to break but we didn't hear a single bird.

We rode bent over the handlebars, concentrating on going as fast as we could. We left town behind and the trees closed in over the road. There was no sign of dawn here and we had to slow a little in the dark.

POP! PSSSSSHHHH.

"Uh-oh," said Frasier, his voice dropping off behind me. "Flat tire."

I slowed and turned back, wishing it wasn't so dark along this stretch. Even though there wasn't a puff of wind, the trees seemed to bend toward us, reaching out with scaly fingerlike twigs.

"Not to worry," said Frasier, kneeling by the bike. "Prepared as always, I have a repair kit."

As he worked, I closed my eyes, trying to feel Jessie.

Since we'd left the tunnel, I'd lost all sense of her. With my eyes shut, I sent my mind out toward Harley Hills, calling for my twin.

But it was no use. She was sealed away from me in the earth and I no longer knew what was happening to her.

I opened my eyes and started to tell Frasier to hurry but the words choked in my throat. The trees really were closer. One branch had dipped down until it was inches from Frasier's head. It was moving strangely.

Oblivious, Frasier was bent over his tire, humming cheerfully as he started to pump it up. Then my eye caught something worse. The woods! Blindly, my hand reached out and grabbed Frasier's shoulder.

"Hey, stop fooling around," said Frasier. "I almost have this tire pumped up."

The branch tipped lower. I wanted to scream out a warning but I couldn't get my throat to work. A leaf brushed Frasier's cheek and he batted at it in annoyance. "Quit it, man," he said.

I pulled at him. Frasier stumbled against me and the branch dipped down where his head had been. "Hey, doofus, what's with you?" he complained.

"They're surrounding us," I croaked.

"Huh? Who?" Finally he looked up. "Wha —?!"

The woods were alive with small glowing red eyes. Thousands of them. Millions! All of them staring at us.

Birds lined the tree branches. The branch near Frasier's head rustled. Startled, he looked up. A bird flapped its black wings as it leaned toward him, pecking with its sharp beak.

"Blah!" Frasier jumped away.

All around us, on both sides of the road, the glowing eyes of the animals began to move closer. And closer.

18

Frasier leaped on his bike, his eyes bugging out. "Let's get out of here!" he yelled, jarring me out of my trance.

I jumped on my bike and screamed after him. But as we pedaled furiously the animals exploded out of the woods into the road. They were after us!

Birds swirled over our heads like black boiling clouds. Squirrels, raccoons, chipmunks, and groundhogs raced after us. Their eyes blazed angrily and they snapped their jaws at our heels.

Huge owls with round fiery eyes swooped at us from out of the trees. I ducked and swerved, and a fat ground-hog leaped at my ankle. It bared its two huge front teeth. As it sank its fangs into my ankle, I kicked out.

The groundhog went flying but the bike skidded and tipped dangerously. I started to lose control. My mind filled with a vision of me lying in the road, being over-run by this horde of demonized creatures.

Desperate, I put out my foot and pushed off the road,

righting myself. Still wobbly, I pedaled harder but the animals surrounded me, nipping at my wheels.

A growling squirrel leaped straight at me. I swung my arm to bat it away but the thing clung to my shirt, its beady glowing eyes fixed on my face.

Panic shot through me like a geyser. I flapped my arm, finally shaking off the squirrel. At that moment a cloud of birds, squawking with fury, swarmed around my head. I couldn't see the road. I couldn't see Frasier.

The birds veered off as another giant owl dove at me. I hunched down over the handlebars and gritted my teeth. Its wings brushed me hard. The bike tipped. The owl slammed me with its other wing.

I struggled furiously to keep my balance but the bike skidded on a patch of sand. My wheels spun out. This time I was really going over. As my hands tore free of the handlebars, I saw the owl swooping down.

I couldn't let it get me! I had to save Jessie! Airborne, I grabbed the handlebars and jerked up. The bike sailed. I landed hard, bounced, but the bike didn't fall.

For an instant I felt elated. I could never do that trick in a million tries. Probably I could never do it again.

I pedaled faster, catching up with Frasier, who was swinging his bicycle pump at the owls and dive-bombing birds. "Faster," breathed Frasier, his face red and his glasses half off. "I think we're going to make it."

He was right. We had outdistanced the ground animals and were getting near the edge of the woods. The birds' attacks already seemed less savage. And finally the last owl hooted in our ears and curled away back into the trees.

Just a little farther and we'd be at the turn into Harley Hills. Nothing lived there. Except the aliens.

We were nearly there when Frasier screamed, "NO!"

I looked past him. My heart slammed against my ribs. The road ahead was completely blocked with porcupines. I'd hardly ever seen a porcupine but here there must have been hundreds.

They had their backs pointed toward us but looked over their shoulders, staring at us with tiny red eyes glowing like red-hot barbecue coals.

"Why aren't they facing us?" I asked as we slowed our bikes, looking for a way around. My stomach felt like it was filled with lead.

"They're pointed for quill shooting," said Frasier.

My stomach sank even farther.

"One porcupine couldn't do that much damage," Frasier mused. "But a hundred of them could make us look like pincushions."

"Any suggestions?" I asked hopefully.

"There's no way around," said Frasier. "We'll have to ride straight at them and hope they don't want to get run over. At least they can't run very fast."

"All right," I said. "Let's stick close together."

We stood on the pedals and rode at the porcupines as hard as we could. It didn't look like they were going to move. Then finally there was a rippling motion.

Frasier's plan, such as it was, was working! The porcupines were waddling out of the way.

But suddenly, "OW!" Something long and sharp hit my shoulder and bounced off. And then the air was filled with deadly porcupine needles.

19

HSSSSSSSS. HSSSSS.

First one bike tire, then another, took a direct hit. I felt a sharp pain in my leg. The bicycle was getting harder to pedal. Frasier's tires were flat, too, porcupine quills sticking out all over them.

"Abandon bikes!" yelled Frasier, vaulting over the front of his handlebars.

My stomach shriveled at the thought of being on foot in the midst of these dart-shooting animals but I knew Frasier was right. I could hardly pedal my bike with its ruined tires. But we could outrun the porcupines.

I jumped off and dropped the bike. Two porcupines scuttled out from under it, shooting quills. One stuck in my arm and I ripped it out as I hurtled over the animals' backs.

Another quill shot past my ear and then I was on clear road. Even as a quill pierced my leg I felt hope that we might make it. I caught up to Frasier and started to pass him. He wasn't moving very fast, I realized.

I grabbed his arm and pulled him along. "Hurry up," I yelled as another volley of quills fell just a few feet behind us.

"Ow. I'm hurt," groaned Frasier.

I pulled him around the turn that led up into the hills and pressed on, ignoring Frasier's moans until I was sure the porcupines were no longer following.

Frasier sank down on a flat rock. "I've got to get to a hospital," he said, stretching out his leg. His face was scrunched up in pain and his glasses were hanging off one ear. "Look at my knee."

Three porcupine quills stuck out of his knee. I worked two more out of my leg, wincing at the pain of the barb. "Just pull them out, Frase," I said. "We've got to get going."

"What if they're poisoned? I don't know anything about porcupine quills," he wailed. "What if I'm allergic? I need a doctor."

"Frasier, to get to a hospital we'd have to go back through the woods," I reminded him. "On foot. It's not a good idea. I pulled mine out. You can do it."

"I can't," he whispered. "You do it for me."

He squeezed his eyes shut and I got all three out as gently as I could. "Thanks, Nick," Frasier said, sniffling a little. "That wasn't so bad."

As he rubbed his knee, I looked around. "Oh, no," I

breathed, the feeling of dread beginning to grow in me again. "It's getting lighter."

"Duh, no kidding," said Frasier, sounding more like his normal self. "That's what generally happens when the sun comes up. It gets lighter."

"It's not the sun," I said. "The sun is over there." Without taking my eyes off the other glow, I pointed east, at a patch of lighter sky where the sun was rising.

Frasier, looking concerned at last, stood and looked north with me. A faint pinkish-yellow glow was growing slowly against the dark sky. The glow was coming from Harley Hill.

20

"Fire?" asked Frasier in a hollow voice.

I shook my head. "Too steady." And too familiar. But I didn't have to say it. We both knew what the glow was.

"How could it be?" asked Frasier, following me as I began to hurry up into the hills. "We just buried them in ten tons of rock. They can't have dug out already."

"Maybe they melted it all," I said gruffly, climbing as fast as I could.

Nothing stirred as we scrambled over rocks and pulled ourselves up boulders. There were no birds, no squirrels, not even a reptile. Nothing moved but I had the awful sense we were being watched.

The only sound was that low hum that seemed to vibrate right through the ground under our feet. The glow grew brighter as we climbed.

Then we reached a ledge that looked out on the tallest of the Harley Hills, the source of the strange glow. Frasier gasped and clutched my arm. My blood turned to ice in my veins.

"They look like ants," breathed Frasier, crouching down beside me.

Hundreds of human adults — all the adults in town, it looked like — were swarming over the rockslide we'd caused. They were picking up the rocks and carrying them away, opening up the cave entrance we'd been so thrilled about burying.

"There's Mom and Dad," I cried, getting a hollow feeling like the aliens had just scooped out all my insides.

Horrified, I watched my parents bend over a large rock and lift it between them. As they stepped away, a beam of pinkish-yellow light shot out of the ground.

"My parents, too," said Frasier in a quiet, fearful voice.

Mrs. Wellington was small and kind of round. Frasier gasped as she bent over and put her arms around a rock that was twice as big as her head.

She tried to stand but the rock didn't budge. She kept tugging and straining at it, refusing to give up.

"My mom doesn't even like to carry the grocery bags in by herself," moaned Frasier. "She has a bad back."

Mr. Wellington was right beside her but he ignored his wife and kept working on his own like a robot.

Finally Mrs. Wellington struggled to her feet, clutching the rock to her chest. She began to stagger across the rockslide, her legs buckling at every step. It didn't look like she was going to make it.

Frasier started to his feet but I pulled him back. "You can't help, Frase," I said. "They're too far away."

He knew I was right. He watched, balling his hands into tight fists, as his mother tottered under her heavy load. Frasier's father brushed past her, carrying his own big boulder. Mr. Wellington dropped his rock on the pile they were making and headed back for more, passing his struggling wife once again.

Frasier groaned through clenched teeth. But his mother didn't fall. She finally dropped her rock and went back for another, passing my parents without a glance.

My mom and dad each carried stones so big I knew they couldn't see where they were going over the uneven slide of rocks. My nerves jumped with every wobbly step they took.

Then a rock slid under my mom's foot. As she slipped, the boulder in her arms went flying. She fell heavily onto the rocks and her own rock landed right on her foot. Dad walked right around her and kept going without even a backwards glance.

Shouting, I jumped to my feet. It was Frasier's turn to pull *me* back. I knew he was right but my blood was boiling. "The aliens are going to pay for this," I vowed.

Frasier nodded. "They've turned our parents into ants," he said angrily. "Ants obey the queen, right? And our grown-ups obey the aliens. Whatever the aliens want, the people do. Never thinking about what might happen to themselves. Or each other. Or their children. They're going to keep digging until they uncover the alien cave. No matter what."

My mother got painfully to her feet. She picked up her boulder again and, limping, continued on her way. It was horrible. Unless —

"What if it's not the alien ship they're after?" I said, feeling a flicker of hope.

Maybe the adults had a real reason to work so hard, whatever the cost to themselves. "Maybe they're trying to rescue my sister!"

Frasier glanced at me. "I don't think so."

21

"Listen, Frasier," I said, turning to him all excited. "One time, when Jessie was little, she wandered off into the woods and got lost. It was getting dark and my parents were frantic. Then the whole town got together and searched until they found her." I smiled, warming to the idea. "It could be happening again."

Frasier shook his head. "You're deluded, dude," he said. "These are just husks of people. They don't help each other. They don't even speak to each other. Do they look like people frantically searching for a missing girl? They're not even calling out her name."

We watched our parents drop their loads of heavy stones and immediately turn back for more. "They're not human anymore, Nick," he said sadly. "And by now Jessie is an alien, too."

I wheeled. Shock traveled through me like a thunderbolt. "Take that back," I shouted, raising my fists threateningly. "Take that back or you're dog meat."

Frasier backed away from me, pushing his glasses up

on his nose. "Sorry, man," he said. "It was just a thought. I didn't mean it."

We watched the adults in silence for a short while longer. Suddenly, as a few more rocks were moved, a large section of the cave was exposed. A beam of light shot up from inside, visible even now that the sun was up.

What Frasier had said scared me as much as it angered me and I felt desperate, not knowing what to do next. I wished I could still sense Jessie, so I would know where she was.

Then I got an idea.

"Let's go down and ask them," I suggested excitedly.

Frasier frowned uncertainly. "Ask them what?"

"Ask them if they're looking for Jessie," I explained. "Even if they're not, they'll know where she is. We'll make them tell us."

Frasier swallowed and looked across to Harley Hill. I knew he was thinking that there were a lot of them and if they wanted to overpower us they could. Then we'd find out where Jessie was, all right. We'd be right there with her. Caught.

"We can outrun them if they start to come after us," I argued. "And we know these hills a lot better than any of them. There's a million places we can hide."

It took us a while to cross to Harley Hill and the rockslide area. When we got there the adults had exposed enough of the cave mouth for a full-sized human to fit through. Pinkish-yellow light poured over them as they worked, making their stiff faces shine like plastic.

We peeked around the side of a tall boulder, working up courage to show ourselves. "Here goes nothing," said Frasier as he stepped out.

Quickly I joined him. We stepped right into the path of Mr. Burgess, our school principal. He was lugging a stone as big as his oversize belly, and his face was pouring sweat.

"Excuse me, Mr. Burgess," I said in a trembly voice, "are all you people searching for my sister, Jessie?"

His head jerked up and his startled eyes widened at the sight of us. He opened his mouth to speak. At first no sound emerged. Then the slithering thing crossed his blank eyes.

And the next second he started making a horrible high-pitched screeching noise. His tongue stuck out and started to whip around like a snake. It was some kind of alarm!

"EEEOOOOOOOEEEEEEEOOOOOOOOOOIIIIIIII!"

The piercing noise was so loud my eardrums started vibrating like they would burst.

The others dropped their rocks and turned toward us. All of them began to march in our direction, hands outstretched.

"Run!" Frasier shouted in my ear. I could barely hear him but it didn't matter because I was already running.

Maybe we should have turned and run back the way we came, but we didn't.

With the adults surging toward us, there was only one other place to run to.

The cave.

We jumped over the low mound of rocks remaining at the mouth of the cave and darted inside. The hum grew louder and all around us the light brightened. I felt bombarded with alien light and that strange hypnotizing noise. At the same time the walls seemed to close in around us.

"Talk about jumping out of the frying pan into the fire," shouted Frasier. His hair stuck up in spikes on his head and his eyes were big behind his lenses.

"Shut up and run!" I yelled, and plunged deeper into the tunnel.

Behind us came the sound of a thousand zombies hunting us down.

22

We ran like the wind, our feet scarcely skimming the cave floor. Our hearts were bursting with the fear of being caught by people we'd known all our lives — people who had been turned into monsters.

My mind flashed with pictures of horror — my parents carrying Jessie through that dark, low tunnel to the aliens, my parents snatching me and Frasier and throwing us into the alien pool where tentacles snapped us up like fish bait.

I was so filled with fear I didn't notice how far we'd run. But suddenly Frasier stopped and leaned against the side of the cave tunnel to catch his breath.

Only then did I notice that there was no sound except for our own heavy breathing and the low alien hum. Nobody was chasing us.

"Why bother coming after us?" asked Frasier, mopping his brow with the end of his shirt. "We're already going where they wanted to take us." He shivered and pulled away from the wall. "I think we'd better go back. We'll find a way past those adults."

But I hardly heard him. I was getting a strong feeling that Jessie was close by. And this time I felt that she could sense me, too!

"We have to go on," I told Frasier. "Jessie's in here somewhere. And she knows that I'm coming. She's waiting for me."

Frasier looked worried. "How do you know?"

"I can *feel* it." I shrugged, helpless to explain. "It's a twin thing. I can't tell you how I know. I just *know*."

Frasier swallowed hard and nodded. I would have understood if he wanted to go back but I was grateful he didn't.

As we went on, I tried not to wonder if we would ever get out of here alive. The tunnel was round and smooth. The rock walls were swirled with colors — purple and gold and blue. It would have been beautiful if we hadn't known the kind of creatures that made it.

The hum seemed to come from everywhere and nowhere. It crept under our skin and seeped into our blood until it seemed like our insides vibrated. I was afraid it would take over our brains, swallow us, and spit out the human part, like it had with our parents.

But the pull from Jessie was strong. I concentrated on that, trying to shut out the hum that threatened to turn my brain into static.

"Nick," Frasier said suddenly. "I just had a bad thought."

"What?"

"Maybe it's not Jessie in your head," he said slowly. "What if it's the aliens, pretending to be Jessie so they can lure us in here?"

A shiver traveled down my spine. "NO," I said, louder than I meant to. "It *is* her. I'm sure."

I might have tried to explain it better but just then we came to a fork in the tunnel. "This wasn't here before!" I said.

Frasier cautiously looked down the new tunnel. It glowed faintly and was the same smooth rock as the one we were walking in. "So these slimy alien creeps created a new tunnel. That's an excellent reason not to go down there."

"You're probably right. But that's exactly what I'm going to do," I said.

"I knew it!" said Frasier.

"Look, Frase, we already know what's at the end of the main tunnel," I said, shuddering at the memory.

I took my first step into the new tunnel. I braced myself, waiting for whatever new blast of alien horror was in store for us.

13

The hum seemed even deeper here. It picked up the beat of my heart, making it thud like a bass drum. And the glow seemed pinker, maybe a little brighter.

But the light still had no source and no temperature. It wasn't warm or cold, it just *was*.

This tunnel was almost exactly like the main tunnel. I realized how easily we could get lost in here, where everything looked the same — smooth and alien.

But nothing happened to us. And I could still feel Jessie, trapped in a dark place where she couldn't move.

"I think she's down here," I said excitedly to Frasier, starting to hurry through the tunnel.

"I hope you're right, man," he said. "'Cause something's down here. Feel that wind?"

As he spoke, a rush of air ruffled over my scalp. I shivered though it wasn't cold and broke into a run. Suddenly I felt I had to find Jessie right away. I felt movement around her, the excitement of alien creatures.

"Hey! Nick! Wait up," called Frasier.

"We're running out of time," I called back. "The things know we're here." My voice echoed: "We're here-ere-ere." It spooked me, sending my heart into a spin.

Suddenly the tunnel ended.

It opened into a huge immense round cavern. The curving dome of the roof towered so high over our heads we had to crane our necks to see it all. The glow seemed brighter up there but we still couldn't see any source.

"Wow," said Frasier, beginning slowly to circle the walls. "Awesome!"

Long, thick stalactite structures came down from the roof and melded into huge support struts. The tops of the stalactites were thick but blurry, almost lost in the glow from the roof.

Strange big twisted structures rose from the floor of the cavern. Some had small protrusions, almost like handles, sticking out of them. There were other protrusions sticking out of the smooth walls.

It was familiar, something like the cavern we'd found at the end of the other tunnel. But this one was much bigger and more organized-looking.

The eerie glow had a menacing feel to it. There was a presence here that we couldn't see. It filled me with dread as heavy as lead.

I didn't think we'd be allowed to walk around here by ourselves for very long.

But Jessie's fear drowned out my own. I could feel her

calling *help me, help me* inside my head. She was very close. I reached out with my mind, trying to find her.

"Metal and rock melted together," Frasier said wonderingly, running his hand over one of the twisty things sprouting from the floor. It rose in a tall, sweeping curve that towered over his head. "It looks like it's supposed to be something. Like it has a purpose."

He ran his hand over one of the odd formations sticking out of the side of the strange structure. "And these things, what are these?"

Suddenly he jerked his hand away and looked around, his eyes widening. "Nick, this is no cavern. This is the UFO itself! The ship that burrowed into the hills!" He stared straight up and the cavern's glow poured down over his awestruck face. "We're inside it, man! Inside the mothership!"

And then another voice shouted right into my ear. "Nick," cried Jessie. "I'm here! Right here!"

24

I whipped around, expecting to see Jessie right behind me. But there was nothing there. Nothing anywhere. Everything was just as it had been, bathed in
pinkish-yellow alien light.

Frasier was staring at me like he was afraid I'd been
possessed by the aliens. "Nick, are you okay?" he asked.
"Didn't you hear what I said about the mothership?
Why are you twirling around like that?"

"Nick, where are you?" cried Jessie's voice again.

I whipped around in the other direction. "Don't you
hear Jessie calling?" I asked Frasier. "She's right here!"

My sister sounded like she was standing next to me.
But I still couldn't see her. I looked around wildly, trying
to figure out where her voice was coming from.

Frasier looked worried. "I don't hear a thing, Nick.
There's nobody here but us." He didn't say it but I could
tell he was scared that the aliens were playing games
with my head. And we all knew who would win those
games.

I whirled as Jessie's voice sounded in my ear again.

"You're too close, Nick," Jessie cried fearfully. *"Be careful!"*

It was no use. I couldn't figure out where she was by listening. Her voice was inside my head. But I knew she was in here, inside the mothership.

They had her hidden but I would find her. I ran to the wall and began banging on it. But it felt as solid as rock.

Then I noticed again the handlelike structures that stuck out of the wall. They might be hatch handles, or doorknobs to other rooms in the ship. In one of those rooms Jessie was being kept prisoner.

Excited and terrified about what else I might find, I grabbed one of the structures and pulled down. It seemed to move a fraction, then stop. It was smooth but kind of sticky to the touch. The feel of it made my skin crawl. It was made for tentacles, not human hands.

But I was sure I had felt it move. Gritting my teeth, I grasped the thing as hard as I could and threw all my weight on it.

"Nick, what are you doing?" yelled Frasier. "Stop! Those look like control levers!"

The "lever" stayed put. I let it go and ran to the next one, wiping my sticky hands on my shirt. My stomach twisted in disgust as my slimy fingers stuck to the cloth. I pulled them free but now my shirt was sticky, too.

The next "lever" was higher. I would have to jump to grab it. I backed up a few feet to get a running start.

"What are you —?" Frasier started to ask. Then I

launched into my sprint and he could see what I was doing.

"NO!" shouted Frasier as my feet left the ground in a spectacular leap. My hands grasped the lever. I winced at the cold stickiness of it.

"DON'T!" yelled Frasier. "If you pull on the wrong one it might —"

My full weight jerked down on the lever. My heart leaped into my throat as the lever moved. It seemed stiff at first, then it slid easily, depositing me on the floor.

With a smooth WHOOSH a huge slab of molten wall began to slide open.

"Get away from there!" screamed Frasier.

"Nick!" shouted Jessie. "I'm here! Right here!"

25

Light poured out of the fissure in the wall, dazzling my eyes. "Jessie!" I cried. "I can't see you. Tell me where you are!"

"Jessie?!" Frasier came up behind me, squinting as he tried to peer into the widening opening. "Is that really you?"

"Be careful!" yelled Jessie. "Don't let them grab you!"

"I hear her, too, Nick." Frasier said excitedly. "She really *is* inside!"

As the wall continued to slide, the glow from within grew brighter, spilling out onto the cavern floor. But I couldn't see through the light. It was like glowing pea soup.

I stepped forward and grabbed the side of the opening to hoist myself inside.

"Nick, wait!" urged Frasier. "They'll get you! You don't know what's waiting in there!"

But I had to go. If the wall closed up again I might

never be able to get inside. Jessie would be trapped with the aliens forever.

I stepped into the glowing fog.

"Be careful, Nick," cried Jessie. "They're coming!"

One leg disappeared into the light, then the other. I couldn't see my arms. The fog of light swirled thickly around me and I realized I couldn't see my hand in front of my face.

I fought down panic and took another step. My foot stuck to the floor. I pulled harder and my foot came away with a loud sucking sound. I felt like I was walking in three inches of thick warm tar. I couldn't see it but I knew it wasn't anything as nice as tar.

Gagging and shaking with fear that something would jump at me out of the light, I pressed on, following Jessie's voice.

"I hear one of them, Nick," she called. "It's coming at you."

I felt a change in the air near my head. It was no more than a shimmer but instinctively I ducked.

WHAAAP!

Something whiplike whizzed over my head. Twisting up, I caught a glimpse of a glowing tentacle as it lashed across the space where my head had been and disappeared into the mist.

Keeping my head low, I kept moving toward the place where I'd heard Jessie. I was afraid to call out to her, afraid to give my position away to the aliens.

Feeling another shimmer in the air, I ducked again and turned to look and —

SNAAAAAP!

The whipping tentacle came so close I fell to my knees. Instantly I felt as if the sticky floor was sucking me in.

"Ewggh," I choked, struggling to free myself. I floundered in the goo, getting myself coated with sticky slime. Just as I got to my feet, a tentacle whipped out of the glowing mist and I stumbled.

Falling, I stuck out my hands, terrified that I would land facedown on the floor and drown in alien slobber. My hands sank to my wrists. My stomach heaved and my heart fought to escape my chest.

I started to push myself up, gasping with fear and disgust. I pulled one hand as hard as I could and slowly — SWUUUCK! — it came unstuck.

But suddenly something dropped onto my free hand. It felt warm and thick, like tapioca pudding. I shook my hand but it jiggled and stuck.

26

The blob slid over my fingertips. I felt it running between my fingers. Frantically, I tried to shake it off and drops spattered onto the gooey floor.

I yanked my other hand free of the floor and scraped at the thing. Finally I managed to fling it off me to the floor. It splattered into a hundred blobby drops.

It must be slime goo that drips off the tentacles, I thought, my flesh crawling.

As the mist swirled I watched the blobs quiver and run together in larger puddles, like spatters in a frying pan. The bigger puddles ran toward each other. The blob was re-forming!

Sticky and shaking, I stumbled away from there as fast as I could. "Jessie!" I called out, forgetting about my fear of giving my position away to the aliens. I was just desperate to find her and get out of this horrible place.

"I'm here," she cried. But her voice seemed to be coming from all directions, echoing off the alien walls I couldn't see.

"Where are you?" I cried, whipping my head around, trying to catch a glimpse of her in the swirling glow of fog.

"I don't know," answered Jessie, her voice high and frantic. "I can't see anything. But I can feel them, Nick. They're coming back for me."

I listened hard and tried to let my twin sense pull me toward her, even though her voice kept bouncing around. "Keep talking," I said. "I'll find you."

The glowing fog was so thick it did strange things to her voice.

"Hurry, Nick. I can feel them messing around in my mind. They can't really get in, yet, but they keep trying. I don't know how much longer I can hold them off. I'm scared, Nick," she said in a breathy voice that pierced my heart.

I felt something blobby ooze up around my foot and kicked out, hearing spatters in the mist. It was hard, struggling across the sticky floor, and my legs were beginning to ache. I couldn't even tell how big this room was.

"I'm coming, Jess," I said, hoping I was moving in the right direction.

"Glad to hear that, Nick," said Jessie. She laughed weakly. "Save me from this and you can have all my desserts for the rest of the year. Promise."

Tears pricked at my eyes. That was just like Jessie, trying to sound brave, to make a joke out of the situation when she was terrified out of her mind.

The terrible truth was, even if we did get out of here, there wouldn't be any more desserts — or any Mom to make them — unless we found a way to defeat the alien invasion.

And how could three kids fight blobby stuff that dissolved and re-formed? How could we stop something that could control human thoughts?

I plodded on over the sticky floor. Each step was an effort, a tug-of-war with the floor.

And I was straining to see through the thick mist, fighting off prickles of anxiety, wondering if I would ever find Jessie or just keep going around in circles until I sank into the goo in exhaustion.

Then suddenly there was a horrible shriek.

"NICK!"

It was Jessie.

They'd got her!

27

I leaped up, blood pounding in my veins. Jessie was close. She was screaming inside my head and suddenly I could feel right where she was.

I turned, homing in on her, and ran, tearing my feet out of the goo with every step, struggling not to lose my sneakers. I was on fire with rage but I still couldn't see a thing in the glowing mist.

BANG!

My head rang with pain. I stumbled backwards, realizing I had run smack into something, headfirst.

"Nick!" It was Jessie. Right in front of me! "Are you all right?"

Laughter bubbled up inside me as I groped for the thing I had hit. How typical of Jessie, to ask if I was okay when she was the one captured by aliens.

"I'm right here," I said. My hand touched something hard. I pulled myself closer and Jessie's face swam up out of the mist. She was in a cage!

The edges of the cage disappeared in the thick glow-

94

ing fog but I could see that it was suspended from the ceiling. The cage swung slightly when I touched it. What I didn't see was a door. There seemed to be no way out of the cage.

Jessie grasped the bars, grinning at me in relief. "Am I glad to see you!" she said. "I know you'll get me out of here, Nick. I know it!"

I tried to smile back but at the moment things looked pretty hopeless. The bars of the cage were made out of what looked like melted rock. They were thick and smooth and felt stronger than steel.

No matter how I pulled or pushed at them, they didn't bend even a tiny bit. I reached through and grasped Jessie's hand. "We'll figure this out," I said, wishing my voice sounded more confident.

Jessie nodded, still grinning at me. Her smooth brown hair was matted and full of tangles but otherwise she looked okay. No bruises or cuts. No slithering motion in her eyes.

I moved around the cage but found no door or lock or any way in. The cage hung several feet over the floor and was constructed of the same melted rock bars on all sides.

"How does this open?" I asked.

"I don't know." Jessie's smile slipped. "I was unconscious. I don't even know how I got here. I just woke up inside this — this cage! Like a wild animal!" Her eyes blazed with anger.

Then she looked over her shoulder fearfully. "One of

those things was just here," she said. "I don't think we have much time. A tentacle poked in right there."

She shuddered and pointed toward the back of the cage as I continued to search for a way to get her out. "It brushed up against me," she said. "And then I felt it probing at my mind. It was trying to find a way in!"

I ran my hands over the bars, looking for any kind of break. But all the bars felt smooth. "There has to be a way to open this thing," I muttered.

Inching away from the cage, I stretched my hands out through the thick mist, searching for a wall where I might find a lever or switch that would open the cage.

"Nick, don't go!" pleaded Jessie. "They're coming back for me. I'm afraid! I won't be able to hold out against them. They're going to take over my mind!"

"I have to, Jess. I'll find a way to get you out of here," I promised. "Trust me. Yell out if they come back."

Jessie choked back her tears. In an instant her face disappeared behind me in the mist.

I groped ahead until my fingers bumped a wall. The wall felt slick, the same as the bars of Jessie's cage — rock that had been melted to make it strong and smooth.

Quickly I ran my hands over it, looking for a switch, listening all the while for the sound of a whipping tentacle or the dripping of alien blobs behind me.

But the wall stayed perfectly smooth. I felt my way along it, hating that I was getting farther away from Jessie.

I froze. Something was creeping near me, slithering over the sticky floor, trying to be quiet. I stayed perfectly still, hoping it would miss me.

pppUUCK, squish, ppppUUCK, squish, ppppU-UCK.

It wasn't going to pass me by. It was headed straight for me, but sooo slowly, one maddening inch at a time. Like a slug. But why so slowly?

Was it feeding as it moved? Was that why there was so much gunk on the floor? Could this whole room possibly be an alien feeding trough?

My mind filled with a picture of Jessie in her cage like Hansel and Gretel at the witch's house. My heart pounded and my stomach churned.

pppUCK, squish, pppUCK, squish, pppUCK, squish.

I squinted into the mist as if that might help me see better, but it didn't. I gritted my teeth and balled my hands into fists.

The disgusting feeding noises stopped.

The air stirred. Had I imagined it? No. I felt the mist swirl slightly against my cheek. Something was there. Staring at me.

I clenched the muscles in my arm, then let go and swung my fist with all my might.

Take THAT, you alien creep.

"OW!" the thing squealed in a human voice.

28

I knew that voice. It was Frasier!

I reached out to keep him from falling onto the goopy floor, hoping that it wasn't really some alien that had stolen his voice.

But my hand grabbed shirt and I gripped Frasier's arm. "Why'd you hit me?" he complained.

"I thought you were one of those *things*," I said.

The mist swirled around us and fear shot up my spine. I'd wasted precious minutes, standing still like a frightened rabbit, imagining THINGS creeping up on me, gobbling goo as they came.

I knew we were running out of time. "Help me. I'm looking for a lever or a switch," I explained, telling him about the awful cage Jessie was trapped in.

I felt him shiver as he joined me, running his hands along the smooth wall. "One of those tentacle things almost got me," he whispered, coming closer so I could see his face through the fog. "But I think I figured out how they find us."

Hope flashed through me even as I explored another stretch of wall and found no switch. "What do you mean?"

"Well, nothing could see through this weird mist, right? And those tentacles don't have eyes, so how does it see?"

Frasier sounded pleased with himself so I didn't point out that we had no idea what alien eyes might look like. And the tentacles were only the tip of the alien. We had no idea what the whole creature looked like.

"How do they find us? That was the problem," continued Frasier. "And I think I solved it."

He stuck his face close to mine and stared until he had my full attention. "The things home in on your thoughts," said Frasier. "They sense your brain thinking. The energy or something."

I blinked doubtfully. But in a weird way it seemed to make sense. We moved farther down the wall. I explored frantically for a switch while Frasier kept talking.

"The way it happened was there was this slimy tentacle coming right at me," explained Frasier, wincing at the memory. "My mind just went blank, phtt, blotto, nothing. The tentacle quivered and whipped around like it didn't know where to go. Like it had lost track of me, see?"

"Okay, great," I said. "But how did you make your mind go blank?"

"I was scared to death, that's how!"

Suddenly there was a bloodcurdling scream.

"They're coming!" Jessie shrieked. "They've got me!"

29

"This way," I shouted at Frasier, plunging back toward Jessie.

The goo tugged at my feet. I heard something slap against the cage, and Jessie cried out in terror.

I plunged forward but it felt like I was running in slow motion. I heard slurping and squishy liquid noises. Nothing more from Jessie but little high-pitched yips of fear or pain.

My heart pounded uselessly. I knew I was going to be too late. There would be nothing left of Jessie except maybe her other sneaker left at the bottom of the cage.

At last the outline of the cage emerged from the mist. When I saw what was happening I totally froze in horror. Behind me, Frasier gasped.

Dozens of slimy writhing tentacles were coiling over the cage. They were so excited that the fog was actually being dispersed by the force of their whipping motion.

Even worse, we could see where the tentacles came from. A huge glowing, pulsing dark blob of goo sat under Jessie's cage. It was bubbling up through the bars of the floor of the cage and tentacles were sprouting from all over it!

Popping from the blob, tentacles slid through the bars like fat growing worms, slithering toward my sister. Jessie was squeezing herself away from them, her eyes wide with terror.

She was also trying to fight them. She made fierce breathy sounds as she stamped on the slimy tentacles, stomping them to bits. Others she slammed against the bars with her fists, squishing them.

The broken pieces of tentacle fell back flipping and writhing on the heaving blob. They made loud gassy noises as they landed, like huge, horrible farts.

But the blob absorbed each piece and a new tentacle emerged from the same spot and poked its slithery way back up through the bars.

Jessie was keeping them off her but I could see it was only a matter of time. She was tiring and there were more and more tentacles every second.

"Ugh," she grunted, stamping on a wiggling purple tip. But she couldn't move fast enough to get the one that was coiling itself around her ankle.

"No," I shouted, running forward to pull the thing off her.

I stuck my arm through the bars as far as it would go. My fingers grasped the wriggling tentacle. It was smooth and strong, sticky and slimy.

My stomach heaved into my throat, choking me. I

pulled with all my might and finally the tentacle came free with a sucking noise. Its tip whipped around, trying to grasp my wrist.

"Urrg," Jessie grunted and brought her foot down on the tentacle, smashing it in two against the bar. The tip went limp and dropped off me, splashing back onto the blob. The rest of it writhed, in pain maybe, and withdrew.

Jessie kept stamping but I felt helpless. Reaching in from outside I wasn't strong enough to do anything but pull the alien tentacles off her so she could stomp them herself. I knew this couldn't go on much longer.

Then the mist dispersed a little more. I saw a sight that stole my breath. It was so horrible I didn't even feel the tentacle that was winding up my arm.

"Behind you!" I screamed.

While Jessie had been fighting off the tentacles coming from the bottom and sides of her cage, others had been sneaking up the back of the cage, gathering at her back where she couldn't see them.

Long and fat and thick as my leg, they were coiling in through the bars, weaving their tips toward the back of her head.

"No!" I shouted, tearing a tentacle off my arm, hardly noticing the slime trail it left behind. I felt so far away. The whole cage was between me and the big writhing tentacles.

Jessie whirled but the tentacles were too fast for her. They swung away so they remained hidden behind her.

The floor goo sucked at my sneakers as I started around the cage. "No," I screamed as one of the tentacles lifted a strand of Jessie's hair and wound around it.

I threw myself on the cage and started to haul myself around the bars. Tentacles wound around my ankles and dragged me back as the cage swung wildly.

Where was Frasier?

"Frasier! Help!" I shouted, but I didn't have time to look around for him.

I kicked my feet against the bars, trying to dislodge the tentacles on my ankles. Freeing one foot, I looked up in time to see a glistening purple tentacle dart in the bars behind Jessie's head and coil itself around her neck.

I struggled desperately but already two more had whipped themselves around her arms so she couldn't fight.

Jessie's eyes rolled in terror. Two more tentacles slipped between the bars. Quick as a flash, they wound themselves around her head, right across her face! Jessie was covered with the things!

But that still wasn't the worst. As the tentacles flattened themselves against her face, their wiggling tips probed into her ears.

My whole body seemed to turn inside out with anger and disgust.

That was how they did it! That was how the aliens got into a human brain! They wiggled their way inside the ear and made straight for the soft brain!

"NO!" I couldn't let it happen. There was only one

thing I could do. I knew it would probably cost me my life but I couldn't watch this happen to Jessie.

I had to attack the blob itself.

I dropped down off the cage, tearing tentacles off me right and left, no longer taking the time to stomp them into the gooey floor.

This was Jessie's last chance and I had little hope that it would work. But I had to try.

I crouched down to look over the greasy, pulsing blob, trying to judge the best place to attack.

There was a spot on the top that looked especially soft. It bubbled and dripped more than other parts. And tentacles seemed to sprout from there thicker and faster.

I braced myself. I wouldn't have more than a second before the blob absorbed me. I'd have to make it good.

Wanting to get everything perfect, I pictured in my mind exactly how I'd attack — ramming the blob, then kicking, punching, and biting as furiously as I could. For as long as I could.

I was hoping the tentacles attacking Jessie would drop off to come back and defend their blob from me.

I tensed, head down, and ran straight at the blob like I was shot out of a cannon!

In my mind I heard it scream.

30

"NOOOOOOO! WAAAAIIIIT!"

Startled, I realized it was Frasier's voice I was hearing, not the death agony of the blob.

"Don't, Nick," he yelled. "I've got it!"

There was a clicking noise and then a rumble of stone.

I was already airborne. It was too late to stop. Inches from my face, the blob was glowing brighter and bubbling feverishly. Goo splashed my skin.

I jerked my head up and arched my back, trying to reverse my leap. My feet swung under me and my heels dug into the floor. Goop welled up around my ankles and I slid to a slow stop, my nose almost touching the blob.

Tentacles writhed wildly around my head as I backpedaled furiously, getting myself covered in floor goo and spatters from the blob.

The sound of grinding stone was louder. I looked up

and stared in amazement as the bars of the cage began to slide open.

"I found the lever," yelled Frasier. He bounded across the sticky floor and grabbed me, pulling me away from the pulsing glow of the blob. "Maybe we can still save Jessie."

The blob glowed even brighter, almost blinding. Dark ooze rose to the surface, bubbled and popped. Globs fell to the floor. More tentacles sprouted — and faster, too — an army of slithery tentacles.

I threw myself at the opening of the cage and hauled myself up. I was almost inside when I felt the tentacles coil around my ankles and squeeze, pulling me back.

Reaching down to tear them off, I saw that every inch of the bulging blob was now covered with small squirming tentacles. They wiggled off it in all directions.

Dozens of them nipped at Frasier's ankles, dozens more launched themselves at me. They were trying to suck us down into the mess of bubbling goo.

Yelling wordlessly, Frasier stomped at the ones that grabbed his ankles while he helped tear the others off me.

Straining to pull against their slimy grip, I worked my way across the floor of the cage toward my sister.

Poor Jessie was huddled in a ball and so plastered with writhing tentacles I could hardly see her.

"Jessie!" I called, beginning to rip the tentacles off her. "Jess?"

No answer.

I pried the tentacles off her face, smashing them against the floor until they lay still.

Jessie's eyes were closed. There were tentacles wound into both her ears! I could see she was unconscious.

But there was one thing I didn't know. Had the aliens eaten her brain?!

I yanked the tentacle tips from her ears and banged them on the bars. They went limp and fell away through the bottom of the cage. I wished I had a weapon — a knife or even a heavy stone — but my fist would have to do.

Working feverishly, I peeled the things from Jessie's hair and off her shoulders and slammed them against the stone bars, wincing against the drops that spattered my face.

The cage swayed as something heavy landed in it. My heart nearly burst with fright. But it was only Frasier, bits of broken tentacle sticking to his feet and legs.

He helped beat back the new ones wriggling up through the bottom of the cage while I got Jessie's arms and legs untangled.

Together we pushed and dragged her out of the cage, beating back more questing tentacles.

We balanced her on the edge of the cage opening so we could kick and stomp the mass of tentacles crawling over the floor, clearing ourselves a path, sort of.

Then, as we lifted Jessie, we noticed the dark blob

was pulsing with bursts of light and boiling over with goo that dripped down its sides and overflowed onto the floor. It jiggled and rocked feverishly, spouting out great clouds of steamy mist.

"I don't think we have much time," said Frasier in a small, shaky voice. "We'd better get out of here."

But even as he spoke the pulsing blob swelled, its bubbling blubber knocking the cage aside. It bulged larger and larger and pulsed harder and harder.

Suddenly, in a huge gassy explosion, the blob erupted like a slimy volcano, spewing hundreds of tentacles and gobs of dark goo into the misty air.

Some of the gobs landed in our hair and on our clothes. They turned instantly to small tentacles and began worming their way down through the strands of hair to our scalps, seeking our ears.

"AAAAAAAAAAAAAAAAA!"

We screamed in revulsion and panic as we grabbed at our hair and clawed at our clothes and stamped our feet.

I plucked wormy tentacles off poor Jessie and flung them against the wall. But when we'd freed ourselves of the small stuff, we noticed what was really happening.

We were surrounded.

Hundreds of tentacles rose from the floor, some higher than our heads, thicker around than even Frasier. Even as we stared, our insides turning to quivering jelly, more tentacles emerged from the mist and joined the crowd, tips quivering like noses in the wind.

They were all around us. I forgot to breathe. My

heart felt like it was trying to rip a hole in my chest. I clutched Jessie closer to me, trying to think how we could get out of this.

Suddenly all of them seemed to come to attention. The tentacle tips stopped quivering. All in unison they swiveled toward us like periscopes.

United, they had homed in on us.

Frasier tapped my shoulder. "Think of nothing," he whispered urgently. "That's the only thing that can save us!"

31

It was the hardest thing I ever tried in my life.

You try it. Just try it. Think of nothing. Make your mind blank. Except that even thinking of thinking of nothing takes some thinking, right?

Jess had it easy — she was already unconscious. What was I supposed to do? Knock myself out?

I glanced at Frasier, feverishly trying to blank my mind and totally aware of how much it wasn't working.

But Frasier's eyes were empty, his jaw slack. His knees were quivering. He was so scared his mind had gone completely blank.

I was terrified to let myself feel that scared. Afraid the tentacles would swallow me and I might never move again.

All together the tentacles swerved toward me and me alone. Waving like hypnotizing snakes, they began to slither across the gooey floor.

My mind howled with fear. Desperately I wanted to run. But there was no way through the army of alien tentacles. My head swiveled, looking for a way out. Finding none.

And then I forced myself to do it. I let the fear grow in me. It was the bravest thing I'd ever done, laying myself open to that paralyzing fear.

I let myself imagine what would happen if the alien tentacles got me and Jessie.

I pictured the wormy things slithering into my ears. How it would tickle as the slimy thing wiggled its way down my ear canal. How its strong tip would slide into my brain.

I felt the aliens eating my mind, gobbling my brain like a hot fudge sundae!

My head filled with slimy tentacles coiling over one another, like a nest of purple snakes, leaving slime trails on the empty inside of my skull.

Until there was nothing in my head but a writhing mass of purple alien tentacles.

My legs began to tremble helplessly as the horror of it washed all thought out of my mind. My blood iced up in my veins and my heart shivered to a stop. Until finally there was nothing left but FEAR.

I was so scared I didn't even know my name.

Slowly the tentacles stopped advancing. Their damp slimy tips wavered in the air, turning every which way. They began whipping around in confusion as if they didn't know which way to turn.

I was so frozen with fear, I didn't notice when the tentacles began to ooze away. Wiggling and searching, they were slowly drawn back into the blob of goo, which had become a shapeless blot on the floor.

As hundreds of tentacles were sucked back in, the blob grew larger again, bulging and bubbling and rippling.

When the last tentacle disappeared with a slurping belch, the blob's glow began to fade. The bubbling subsided and finally stopped.

The blob drooped and lost its shape. It seemed to shrink, little by little. But it wasn't shrinking. It was sinking into the floor.

It seeped down right through the rock, finally vanishing with a faint hiss. All that was left behind was a dark stain in the slime.

The alien was gone.

But we weren't out of here yet. And our minds were paralyzed with fear.

32

"Nick!"

My head jerked. Frasier was shaking me. Light and color flooded back into my brain. My knees felt weak.

"Run for your life!" yelled Frasier. He grabbed Jessie's legs and we started into the thickening mist.

"Hey! Let me go," yelled Jessie, coming awake with a start and kicking out with her legs.

"It's us," I told her. "Me and Frasier."

Coming to herself, Jessie looked around at the swirling mist and caught a glimpse of the cage, its door hanging open. She shivered and grinned at me. "Thanks," she said.

Frasier grabbed her arm. "Let's go!"

We ran into the glowing fog, unable to see through the dense mist, hoping we were headed the right way. We huddled together, alert for whipping tentacles, moving as fast as we could over the gloppy floor.

"Here it is!" cried Frasier triumphantly, somewhere in front of me and Jessie. "I've found the opening."

We hurried after him and emerged into the cavernous mothership. After the clinging, blinding fog of the chamber we'd been in, it seemed even vaster than I remembered.

"Wow." Jessie craned her neck in fearful amazement. "It's humongous."

"Don't stop now," warned Frasier. "We've still got to make it all the way back through the tunnel."

We started running across the huge expanse of the cavern floor, feeling small and terribly visible.

As we circled the towering structures that curved out of the center of the floor, Jessie frowned and slowed.

"I'm getting the strangest feeling from those things," she said between breaths. "Like I almost recognize them. It's creepy."

The hair prickled on my scalp when she said that. "I think those are the pilot's and copilot's seats," I told her. "Maybe they carried you through here at some point. Maybe you were half-conscious."

"Could be," said Jessie, shuddering at the thought of being carried by those tentacles. "Or maybe they just remind me of a modern sculpture I saw at a museum one time."

Jessie picked up the pace again but suddenly Frasier faltered and I ran smack into him.

"Where is it?" Frasier asked breathlessly. "Where's the tunnel?"

I looked. The walls were smooth and seamless, ex-

cept for the odd protrusions of knobs and controls, like
the one that had opened Jessie's chamber.

"I know it was here," said Frasier, his voice rising with
fear. "But it's been closed up! We're trapped!"

I ran up to the wall where the tunnel opening had
been and drummed my fists against it. It was as slick as
marble. I whirled around, my eyes searching along the
cavern wall. Maybe we'd remembered wrong. Maybe
the opening was in another place.

But it wasn't. The aliens had us right where they
wanted us. Trapped inside the mother ship.

I couldn't stand it. A bomb of fury seemed to explode
inside my head. "There has to be some way to open it
up again!" I said, and began to yank on every weird-
looking structure I could reach.

"I don't like this," said Frasier, biting his lip. "You'll set
off an alarm. They'll know we're here."

"They know anyway," I said, hanging my full weight
off a hook-shaped thing that wouldn't move.

"Hey, guys, look at this!" called Jessie from partway
across the room.

I twisted around to look over my shoulder and as I
did the hook-shaped thing moved. The sound of stone
grinding on stone filled the cavern.

"I did it!" I yelled, dropping to the floor. "Let's go."

I turned toward the wall where our tunnel had been.
The wall hadn't moved. The tunnel opening wasn't
there.

"YEEEOOW!" screamed Frasier.

I whipped around. A different section of wall was sliding open. Inside the opening was a pulsing pink blob. It began to ooze down over the floor, raining pink spatters.

"Oh, no!" screamed Jessie. She wasn't looking at the pink blob. Her horrified eyes were staring at the place we'd come from — the cage chamber.

I snapped my eyes around. The chamber wall had closed. But that wasn't what horrified Jessie.

Through the solid rock wall something dark was oozing. At first I almost missed it. It was just a trickle.

But then it began to gush and bubble. The blob!

It poured over the floor, bulging and pulsing madly.

Frasier screamed and began to run. A huge tentacle shot out of the dark blob. It snaked across the broad floor so fast it was a blur.

Frasier glanced behind him and screamed again. It was aiming straight at him, faster than a speeding train. He was running too hard to remember to blank his mind.

I wasn't sure it would have worked this time anyway. Quick as the lash of a whip, the tentacle swept Frasier up off the floor and held him up, coiled in its grasp. Frasier struggled like the lady in King Kong's fist.

The blob began to suck the tentacle back in. Frasier's eyes popped in horror. I could see when his mind went blank with fear but it didn't help now that the alien already had him.

"We'll save you, Frase!" shouted Jessie.

We both took off running, determined to rip Frasier from the alien's grasp. But we had forgotten about the pink blob.

As we pounded across the floor past the big alien structures, it spurted out a pale tentacle, which scooped Jessie off her feet before she even knew it was there.

I skidded to a halt, reversing direction toward my twin. Jessie dangled from the pale tentacle, kicking and screaming.

The tentacle was so pale a shade of pink that it was almost clear, like the biggest, most disgusting jellyfish I had ever seen. It waved Jessie around like it didn't know what to do with her. Or like it was mocking us with how easy we were to catch.

I rushed toward Jessie, my mind filled with rage. Then Frasier whimpered behind me and I hesitated. My eyes darted wildly between my friend and my sister.

I couldn't save them both. I had to choose.

And then I knew with terrible certainty that I couldn't save either one. The aliens were too strong for me. And this was their place, full of their secret things.

Suddenly I had a brainstorm. Sure it was their place. But maybe I could mess it up a little. Maybe I could make them *want* to get rid of me and my friends.

Seething with anger, I turned my back on both weaving, taunting tentacles. I was close to the big structures that I thought controlled the ship. Now was my chance to find out if they really did.

I picked out the biggest structure, thinking that was probably the pilot's cockpit, and dashed for it. I scrambled up, bracing myself for the tentacle that would pluck me away.

As I climbed I banged, pushed, and pulled on every knob and switch I could reach.

At first I didn't hear much except the sound of stone grinding on stone in some distant place elsewhere deep in Harley Hill. That wasn't much help.

I risked a glance back. The dark blob was pulsing wildly and shaking poor Frasier like a rag doll. The pink blob swelled and shrank and bubbled. It was reeling Jessie in slowly, like a fish.

But then I yanked something and there was an earth-shaking noise like ten million cherry bombs all going off at once.

VVVVVVRRRRROOOOOOOOMMMMM!

Ready or not, the mothership was taking off!

33

VVVVVVRRRRROOOOOOOOMMMMM!

I toggled the switch down and the sound responded.

vvvvrrrRRRROOOOOMMMM! vvvvvvrrrrroooo-OOOMMMM!

"Let my friends go," I screamed. "Or I'll destroy your ship and everything in it."

The tentacles waved wildly.

"Way to go!" screamed Jessie, waving a fist in the air.

"Yeah!" Frasier responded slightly less enthusiastically.

"LET THEM GO NOW!" I hollered.

Still the tentacles only writhed uncertainly.

Furious, I banged the heel of my hand on the switch. VVVVVRRRRRROOOOOOOM!

The pink blob dropped Jessie and retracted its tentacle like a rubber band. The blob itself began to retreat back into its chamber.

I had to push the switch one more time before the dark blob released Frasier.

Then both of them ran to me and climbed to lower parts of the pilot's "chair."

"That was *so* cool," said Jessie, grinning.

"Yeah, Nick," said Frasier, reaching up to slap me five. "I thought I was blob food."

I looked toward the dark blob. It was boiling and pulsing light and belching out fog. Tentacles kept popping out and retreating, like it was having trouble controlling itself. It looked mad.

"We're not out of this yet," I told them. "We still don't have a way out of here."

"Maybe you should push that switch again," suggested Frasier eagerly. "Tell them to open the tunnel."

"I don't know that I could get them to understand," I said. "Besides, now that you guys are safe, I don't really want to take any more chances on blowing this thing up."

"But I *found* a way out," said Jessie. "Right before Nick opened the door to that pink one and everything started happening. I never got a chance to show it to you. Over there."

She pointed to what looked like a shadow on the smooth wall.

"It's a crack," Jessie explained. "It goes through to the outside. I felt regular earth dirt when I put my arm through."

"Wow," said Frasier. "That must be one of the places that got damaged in the landing. Wonder why they didn't melt it over?"

Jessie shrugged. Frasier didn't really expect an answer.

"Now all we have to do is get there," I said.

They looked up at me questioningly.

"What's to stop the blob from capturing us as soon as we leave this pilot's seat?" I asked.

Frasier and Jessie looked at each other, realizing we were still trapped.

"There's only one thing to do," I announced.

Jessie tossed her matted hair off her face and looked at me with narrowed eyes. "What?" she asked suspiciously.

"You two run for the crack," I said quickly. "I'll stay here till you're both through, then I'll follow."

Frasier squared his shoulders and pushed up his glasses. "I'll stay," he said bravely.

I shook my head. "I'm the fastest runner. I'll do it."

"But —" Frasier began.

I cut him off. "No arguments. They must already be plotting their next move. We don't have much time."

"He's right," said Jessie. "If one of them tries to attack while Nick's running we can come back out. One of us will make it this far. They'll have to let us go or we'll blow their whole ship up."

"Go," I insisted. But I have to admit my stomach twisted as they dropped off the big stone seat and raced for the crack Jessie had found.

I looked at the dark blob. It rocked and bulged. Fog boiled off it. Tentacles burst out of one spot, then another, but each time the blob sucked them back.

Jessie and Frasier slipped into the shadowy spot and disappeared. "Okay, Nick," Jessie shouted. "Run for it."

I took a deep breath, jumped, and hit the floor sprinting. I put down my head and pumped my arms, trying to ignore the cold spot twitching between my shoulders.

"Faster," screamed Jessie. "It's coming!"

34

Somehow I poured on even more speed. But it seemed to take forever to cross that long stretch of emptiness.

A puff of mist fell over my head and shoulders.

Finally Frasier's arm snaked out of the crack in the ship wall and grabbed me. The crack was narrow and I scraped my ribs diving inside.

Something wet slapped the rock above my head. Frasier winced. His face was white. "Tentacle," he said, pulling me farther inside.

It was dark back there, especially with Frasier blocking out the glow that came from the cavern.

He crouched and a little of the alien glow spilled through the crack. I saw Jessie crawl off into the dark.

My heart lurched and I lunged after her. Frasier grabbed the back of my shirt.

"We found a trapdoor!" said Jessie like it was the neatest thing ever. She hooked her fingers in a rusted iron ring and pulled on the old wooden door. It came up slowly, creaking loudly, like it hadn't been opened in years. Spiderwebs hung off it.

"It's a mine shaft," said Jessie excitedly, ducking her head inside. "Look, there's even a ladder. A real ladder for human feet."

"I don't like it," said Frasier. "We'll only be going deeper underground."

Jessie lowered herself over the edge, onto the ladder. "It feels strong enough," she said, going down.

"She's right," I told Frasier. "It's our only chance."

"Hey, guys! I found an old oil lamp," Jessie yelled happily from below. "And some matches, too." Almost immediately a soft glow of normal earthly light drifted up the shaft. It was beautiful.

Frasier sighed and looked around like he might find some alternative route. But at last he put one foot gingerly on the ladder.

"I hate ladders," he said and then stiffened. "What's that?"

I heard a scraping noise on the stone behind us. And hissing sounds were coming from the cavern.

Frasier froze. I risked a glance behind me. A tentacle was probing along the crack, exploring it.

But something else was blocking the alien light from the cavern. I craned my neck to see out through the crack.

It was the blob creature! It was coming toward us! It oozed and bubbled across the cavern floor faster than I would have thought possible.

"Quick, Frasier," I shouted, jumping down onto the ladder next to him.

He stood frozen for another second. But the slurping, burping sounds were coming closer. And then another tentacle — WHAP! — slammed into the crack.

Frasier let out a yell and flopped onto his belly, wriggling down the ladder. I pushed on his head and grabbed for the iron ring to close the trapdoor.

"Hurry," shouted Jessie.

A tentacle slithered through the crack and whipped straight at us.

I flinched and missed my grip on the trapdoor ring.

The tentacle quivered and began to dive toward me. I grabbed the ring and jerked on the door.

The door stuck. The slimy tentacle glommed onto my wrist and instantly coiled around it. It tore my fingers off the ring.

Frasier pushed up in front of me. He grabbed the tentacle and tugged with all his strength.

SNAP!

It came free and I was jerked backward. I teetered, wheeling my arms, then grabbed the ladder.

"Urggh," Frasier gurgled.

Jessie screamed, "It's got him!"

I looked up. The tentacle was wrapped around Frasier's neck. It was pulling him up out of the shaft.

"I've got his feet," yelled Jessie. "Get it off him!"

But I couldn't reach that high. Frasier was half out. His eyes were bulging and his tongue stuck out.

He was strangling!

35

Frasier's feet kicked feebly.

"I can't hold him!" cried Jessie. "It's too strong."

I gripped Frasier's arm and hauled myself up. His eyes were rolling horribly. Strangling noises were coming from his throat.

The slimy tentacle was wound completely around his neck and the tip was probing up the side of his head toward his ear.

Using Frasier's shoulder I pushed up, jumped, grabbed onto the tentacle, and hung on it with all my weight.

It didn't release its hold even slightly. I felt the strength of it pulsing under my hands.

But then I realized it was stretching! I was pulling Frasier back down inside the shaft!

If I could only get his head below the door! "Pull on his feet again, Jessie," I called down.

Immediately Frasier dropped another few inches. The tentacle was stretching, stretching. I could feel its slimy skin getting tighter as Frasier sank lower into the shaft. But Frasier was gurgling, unable to speak as the tentacle tightened around his throat.

Finally, I gritted my teeth, hoping I wouldn't fall into the shaft, and chinned myself up on the tentacle, keeping my eye on the door ring.

With the last of my strength, I leaped up and grabbed the ring with one hand, dropping my weight onto that arm.

The door popped free and fell with a massive crash.

SQUUI — SPLAT!

The tentacle was severed.

Frasier fell against the ladder unconscious, the limp tentacle end still wrapped around his throat.

"Help me get him down," I called to Jessie.

Together we maneuvered Frasier down the ladder to the floor of the shaft. We propped him against the wall, catching our breath.

The light of the old rusted lamp cast flickering shadows on the dirt walls.

"Ugh!" cried Jessie, pointing, her mouth working soundlessly.

Exhausted, I looked at Frasier. Only then did I notice that the tip of the tentacle was stuck inside his ear!

I lunged forward to pull it out but suddenly Frasier jerked upright.

"You-must-obey," he said in a deep, menacing, robotic voice. "Listen."

Then he slumped back against the wall again, looking shocked but awake. Feeling my stomach rise, I snatched the tentacle out of his ear and flung it against the wall. It fell limply to the floor like a bag of jelly and didn't move.

"What did it mean?" Frasier asked wonderingly in his own voice.

Jessie was holding her hands against her head. "I don't know," she said. "But I felt a nudge in my head. Like — like —"

She shuddered and shook her head hard. "Let's get out of here," she said. "I don't want to think about it. I just want to get as far from these things as we can."

Frasier nodded and climbed unsteadily to his feet. "Where are we? Anybody know?"

Jessie lifted the lamp. "If you look close you can see the label. 'Harley Mine,'" she read, pointing it out.

"The old Harley Zinc Mine," I said wonderingly. "That's been closed for nearly a century."

Frasier shivered. "I hope we can find a way out."

"Why didn't the alien smash its way through the trap-door and follow us?" asked Jessie suddenly. "They melted a whole spaceship into the mountain, what's the big deal about following a few humans down a little old mine shaft?"

"Maybe they're allergic to zinc," I said.

"Yeah," said Frasier. "Or maybe that blob is melting its way through that rickety wooden door right now. I vote we get out of here."

My head jerked up in alarm. Staring up the dark shaft I imagined black goo bubbling through the old wooden door like tar. I scrambled to my feet. "Let's go."

We scurried off into the low tunnel with Jessie in the lead, carrying the lantern. For a long time my attention was concentrated on what was behind us rather than what was ahead.

I kept listening for sounds — the blob's bubbling belches or the slurp and snap of tentacles. But nothing came after us. Nothing I could hear or see, anyway.

I started noticing more about the tunnel we were in. It wasn't smooth, like the alien tunnels.

Instead it was rough, carved out of rock and dirt with pick and ax. By humans. We could see the marks their tools had left.

And every once in a while we came to an area shored up by old timber supports. The timbers were thick but old and rotten. These supports no longer stood straight but leaned and buckled under the weight of earth and rock. They looked like they would topple at a touch.

We moved gingerly around them and went on. Jessie kept lifting the lantern in hopes of sighting some end to the tunnel.

"I think we're still going downhill," Frasier said nervously after a while. "I've been all over Harley Hills and never discovered a mining tunnel. I think the openings to the outside have all been closed up." Frasier's voice rose fearfully. "I think we're trapped in here."

"Zip it, Frasier," snapped Jessie, holding the lamp up

and squinting into the dimness beyond. "Every step we take is a step farther from those alien horrors."

But just then the arch of timber supports we were passing under creaked and shuddered ominously. We hurried past and hunched our shoulders, expecting the mountain to crash in on top of us.

A few rocks fell behind us and we pressed against the side of the tunnel, not daring to breathe. We heard rumbling deep in the hill. Somebody whimpered.

Suddenly there was a sharp CRACK!

One of the supports gave way and the rock wall caved in with a thundering noise. A flood of dirt followed, thickening the air.

When the rumbling stopped, Jessie lifted the lantern. The tunnel behind us was completely blocked.

"At least the aliens can't follow us now," I said, coughing at the thick dust in the air.

"The only way we can go is forward," said Jessie. "Carefully."

We kept to the center of the tunnel, walking as lightly as we could. I tried to keep from thinking of all the tons of rock and earth above us, held up by nothing much.

We walked on for a long time, losing track of whether we were going uphill or downhill. Every time there was a shower of dirt or a few pebbles dislodged and rolled, my heart leaped into my throat and my stomach shriveled to a hard knot.

Then two things happened.

The lamp began to flicker and smoke. "It's almost out of fuel," said Jessie in a frightened whisper.

And the second thing was, the old mining tunnel came to an abrupt end.

But there was no light at the end of this tunnel.

36

Jessie held up the lamp to inspect the wall blocking the tunnel. The feeble light guttered.

"It's a dead end," breathed Jessie. "No way out."

The lamp flickered once more and died.

Frasier wailed into the blackness. "This is it," he moaned. "End of the line. We're going to die like rats in here. No one will ever know what happened to us."

"Shut up, Frasier," Jessie hissed.

"Come to think of it, I'd rather have my brain eaten by aliens," Frasier babbled on. "At least it would be quicker. But we don't even have that choice. We can't get back!"

How could it end like this? I ranted silently. My heart pounded like a hollow drum. We'd been through so much. Bursting with frustration, I shoved at the wall that was our doom, slamming my weight into it.

It moved.

For an instant my mind went blank. Then prickles of

hope began to break out all over my skin. But — could I have imagined that the wall moved?

I shoved it again, putting my shoulder into it. It made a deep scraping noise.

RRRRRRRUUU!

"What was that?" exclaimed Jessie.

"The tunnel's caving in!" cried Frasier.

"No," I said. "Come and help me push. This isn't a dead-end wall. It's a door."

"What!?"

"Really!?"

In our eagerness we stumbled against each other in the dark. Dirt cascaded down on our heads. We all got quiet again. Then we lined up against the wall, shoulders in.

"PUSH!" I ordered.

The massive door slowly creaked open, showering us with clods of dirt and pebbles. Faint light seeped in from the other side.

As soon as it was wide enough we slipped through.

"Wow," I breathed, hardly believing my eyes.

I knew this place. I'd been here before, many times.

"We're in our own basement," Jessie exclaimed.

"Let's get out of here," said Frasier.

We headed for the stairs, passing the huge mounds of dirt Mom and Dad had made digging the other tunnel. The basement door at the top of the stairs stood open and light filtered down over us.

We rushed up the stairs into the light. It was no alien glow this time but good old Earth sunlight.

Stumbling into the kitchen, we kept going. We flung open the back door and ran outside, lifting our faces to the sun and breathing in the fresh air.

For a moment the three of us felt totally at peace. It seemed like we had the whole town to ourselves. There wasn't a soul around.

Not a person, not an animal, nothing. For a long while we didn't speak.

Then Jessie sighed. "What are we going to do?" she asked.

"We need a plan," said Frasier. "We have to figure out some way to save our parents and the other folks. The only way to do that is to get rid of the aliens."

My eye caught a movement in the street out front. I jerked to attention, my heart beginning to race again. "Right now there's only one thing we can do," I said urgently.

"What?" asked Frasier.

"Hide!" I said, jumping to my feet. "They're coming back."

THE MAGIC IS THEIRS.
THE POWER IS YOURS.

by John Peel

WITNESS THE NEXT DIMENSION!

Score, Renald, and Pixel are twelve-year-olds
with magical powers. None knows any world but
his or her own — until they are kidnapped by
strange and sinister forces and plunged into
Diadem, the circuit of all worlds. There they must
use magic and knowledge to survive...and to com-
plete the task for which they've been fated.
And they need *you* to help them....

DIA297